The Parasite Person

The Parasite Person

CELIA FREMLIN

PUBLISHED FOR THE CRIME CLUB BY

DOUBLEDAY & COMPANY, INC.

GARDEN CITY, NEW YORK

1982

The quotation from THE SCIENCE
OF LIVING, by Alfred Adler, is printed
with the permission of George
Allen & Unwin Ltd.

Library of Congress Cataloging in Publication Data

Fremlin, Celia.
The parasite person.

"Crime Club novel."
I. Title.
PR6056.R45P3   1982   823'.914
ISBN 0-385-18300-3
Library of Congress Catalog Card Number 82–45394

First Edition in the United States of America

The Parasite Person

CHAPTER 1

"It was a cry for help," the young woman told him, nestling contentedly against her pillows. "Suicides nearly always are, aren't they, and that's what mine was. So come on. Help me."

Martin raised his eyes from his notebook and looked at his subject uneasily. This wasn't the idea at all.

"Look," he said, "I'm not a social worker. I thought they'd explained to you? This is *research* that I'm doing. I'm working in the Department of Social Psychology on a research project about depression, and it would be of the most enormous help to us if you'd . . ."

"I don't want to be of enormous help to you. Why should I? *I'm* the one who attempted suicide—right? And so *I'm* the one who ought to be helped. Not you."

From the well-stocked fruit-bowl on her bedside locker, she selected a nice plump grape and popped it into her mouth, watching him the while beneath lowered lids. He fumbled with his papers, trying to find her record sheet.

"Ledbetter, Ruth. Aged 19, unemployed. Formerly Psychology student at Mendel College, dropped-out during second year. Admitted to hospital 2.30 a.m. on Monday Feb 2nd having ingested massive overdose of Mogadon . . ."

Mogadon. That labelled it phoney, right from the start. Everybody knows—well, a psychology student, even a dropped-out one, certainly should—that it is virtually impossible actually to kill yourself with Mogadon. In fact, the whole thing was quite splendidly typical, almost a text-book case. Typical age, typical restless life-style, typical choice of non-lethal drug. It should have been a marvellous interview, if only she'd be more co-operative. After so inauspicious a start, Martin wondered if it was worth while going on? If she was going to act up like this, expecting to have her answers wheedled out of her syllable by syllable, it might be better to scrap her here and now. Chalk her up among the "Don't Knows" and be done with it?

"Well?" she said. Her pale, pointed little face, still yellowish from the overdose, was tilted challengingly in his direction, and with this small bit of encouragement Martin decided to plough on.

"Look," he began, "Look . . . er . . ." (*What* was the damn girl's name? Ruth. That was it.) "Look, Ruth, I don't want to worry you if you'd rather be left alone; but if you *could* bring yourself to answer just one or two questions. Like—well . . . What actually was it that finally drove you to this . . . well . . . this very drastic . . . ?"

"Can't you say 'Suicide'? You suffer from a lisp, or something? 'Suicide, suicide, suicide!' Go on, *say* it! That's why you're *here*, for Chrissake, because I'm a suicide! That's the only reason why you're talking to me at all. It's a bit late in the day to be pretending you've never heard of the word!"

Frowning slightly, Martin took it all down verbatim. There was no way this was going to fit into any of his categories, but at least she was talking, that was the main thing. He set himself to probe further, using the method proper in a depth-interview, which is to follow along the lines which the subject himself has opened up.

"'Suicide,' then. You're quite right, we should be talking frankly to each other. Your suicide attempt, okay? Would you say it was a sudden decision—a sudden uncontrollable impulse? Or had you been depressed for some time . . . ?"

"Depressed? Who's talking about being depressed? I wasn't depressed in the least. I was just into suicide, that's all."

Martin frowned yet more deeply, but he kept his cool—his scientific detachment, as he liked to regard it.

"Into suicide," he repeated, in the correct depth-interview manner, quoting her own words back at her in a neutral, non-judgemental sort of tone. "And what was it, would you say, that got you 'into suicide' in the first place?"

"Oh." She pondered for a moment. "I think I mostly wanted to get into something that there wasn't an Evening Class in. It's not so easy these days. They've got Tarot cards already, you know, at the Houndsditch Institute, and I'm told they're starting Levitation in September. You have to go so far to be way-out these days that over the edge is where it's at."

"'Over the edge is where it's at,'" Martin repeated gravely, scribbling away in his notebook while he spoke; and then, the non-judgemental stance cracking for a moment, he found himself protesting: "But you know, Ruth, you can't go in for suicide like you go in for yoga. It's—well—it's too final."

"Too final for who? Look, Prof, if I'm into suicide I'm into finality, aren't I? I tell you, I'm hooked on finality like it was Valium, they can't get me off it. And like they said, don't mix it with alcohol. And so I did mix it with alcohol, and did I take off! Wow! That was *something!* It really was! Eeeee . . . eeeeee . . . !"

These last sounds, with their shrill, long-drawn-out note of glee, were impossible to transcribe in shorthand, and so Martin left a space for them, hoping that he would remember, when the time came, what the space stood for. In the days when he'd done his own typing, this sort of thing hadn't mattered so much; but now that he had moved in with Helen, who loved him so passionately, and who strove so earnestly to be the sort of help to him in his career that his wife had never been, it was a little bit more complicated. Adorably, she had taken over the typing-up of his interviews as her own special chore, and so anxious was she to get everything exactly right that it was really quite an embarrassment at times.

"Is this 'perverted' or 'parental'?" she would worriedly inquire, and for the life of him he could hardly ever tell. Nor could he bring himself to explain to her—so conscientious was she, and so full of faith in him—that honestly it didn't matter a damn, either would do, an interview was an interview, and the important thing was to have sixty-four of them in the bag before May 4th.

May 4th. Barely three months away now, and already he was badly behind schedule. Less than a dozen interviews completed so far and more than fifty still to come.

Concentrate, Martin, concentrate, get the damn thing *done*. One more is one more. . . .

"'Finality,'" he repeated, picking up her key word in the approved manner. "Even the finality of death, would you say? Your own death?"

"Look, Prof, Death is the in-thing, didn't you know? Don't they tell you these things up there among the brain-freaks? Death is *in*, brother! Death is the Now-thing. Up-to-the-minute, fat-free, problem-enriched Death. Watch out for it on the Commercials: Death Dyes Whiter. 'Well, they *said* anything could happen,' remarks the blonde in the bikini when she finds herself standing before the Throne of God. . . ."

Martin hadn't got half of this down. It was always harder when they went off the beaten track like this. His shorthand speeds, acquired rather late in life, were better adapted to those interviews where the subject answered as he was expected to answer, the sentiments falling easily and naturally into one or other of Martin's five carefully-thought-out categories.

Not that he *wanted* all his subjects to give the expected answer, not really. On the contrary, like any other social scientist, he lived in hopes of turning up results so startling, so unprecedented, as to turn establishment assumptions right on their heads. Perhaps he would even end up on television, putting some revered celebrity or other firmly in place in front of millions of viewers. . . .

Or at least (less ambitiously) he hoped that *something* a lit-

tle bit new might turn up; something which might—just *might*
—open up some area of research which hadn't already been
picked clean by hordes of predecessors in the field.

So, "Just a minute," he said, and scribbled ferociously to
catch up. Now he came to write it down, he was beginning to
realise that she hadn't really told him anything at all. Despite
all this self-display, she had in fact revealed nothing of her
problems. She had answered none of his questions, and had
thrown no light whatsoever on the real motives for her suicide
attempt. And as for depression, which was what the whole survey was supposed to be about, she had simply denied it.

Oh well, Never mind. At least there were some good quotes
here. Good quotes can always be dragged in somehow, somewhere.

On, then, to Question Five. Few of them could resist this
one, even if they'd been a bit sticky earlier on:

"Do you feel there was anyone in your circle who could
have helped you through this bad patch if they'd been
more caring . . . more understanding . . . ?"

"Like who?" She looked at him guardedly. "What are you
getting at?"

What indeed? Martin played for time, scribbling energet-
ically. "Well: what I really meant was, isn't there anyone
among your friends who . . . ?"

"*Friends!* Oh, you're talking about *friends*. You didn't say.
Look, Professor, I got friends like you got dandruff—just for
brushing-off, kind of thing."

Had he got dandruff? Nervously, Martin tried to glimpse the
shoulders of his dark suit, swivelling his eyes round so far that
he felt as if he'd sprained them.

He couldn't see a thing. He'd have to examine the suit later.

"Just one or two more questions, Ruth, and then we'll be
through. I don't want to tire you, my dear, or pry into areas of
your life that may be painful; but have you—how shall I put
it?—have you a partner? A sex partner—a boyfriend?"

"Like I told you. Dandruff. You suffering from amnesia, or something?"

"I'm sorry . . ." Martin's eyes swept uneasily over the final three questions, all of which presumed some kind of affirmative reply to Question Six. Did you confide in him? Do you feel that he could have helped you more than he did? Do you feel that he let you down in any way?

Mostly, they opened up like flowers in springtime to these sort of questions, pouring forth griefs, resentments, hang-ups that could be dealt out like a pack of cards under his prescribed headings. Guilt, Hostility, Self-Justification, Revenge—there was a slot for everything.

But no slot for Dandruff. The computer wouldn't be able to handle it. Martin sucked the end of his biro, and decided to bring the thing to a conclusion.

"Now, Ruth," he said, putting a sort of penultimate note into his voice to show her that the end was near, "I'm very grateful to you indeed for answering all these questions." (Actually she hadn't answered a single one of them, but let that pass.) "It's been most interesting. Now, before we finish, is there anything *you* would like to ask *me?*" A cunning one, this. It was surprising how often it released not a question, but a whole new batch of confidences.

But not this time. The girl looked him up and down warily, then took up the challenge.

"Tell me how you got me?" she demanded. "I mean, so okay, you're out collecting suicides like a kid collecting conkers. But why *me?* We're all death-freaks in this ward, you know, we've all had a go. So what made you pick on me in particular?"

Because you're a C-class female, under twenty-five. Because you've been under treatment for depression at least once during the past two years. Because this hospital you're in doesn't take me too far out of my way. Because the psychiatrist who runs the Thursday clinic happens to be an old acquaintance of mine and so he lets me have the odd peek at his confidential records . . .

"It's a special technique known as Random Sampling," Martin explained blandly. "It's a bit too technical, I'm afraid, for the ordinary layman, but . . ." He let his voice tail away, and began shuffling his papers together, indicating that the interview was at an end.

"Well, goodbye, Ruth," he said, standing up with an air of finality and holding out his hand. "It's been a great pleasure meeting you, and I'm most grateful for all your help. I expect you'll be out of here in a day or two, eh?"

She should have taken his outstretched hand by now, and be murmuring words to the effect that *she* was the one to be grateful . . . a chance to get it off her chest . . . feeling better already . . . that sort of thing. The big, hearty smile with which he had started his little speech was drying on his face; and still she made no move.

"*Why* do you expect I'll be out of here in a day or two?" she inquired. "You don't know anything about it. For all you know, my liver might start playing up again." It sounded like a threat.

"Ah. Well." Martin was at a loss for a suitable reply. What *do* you say about a liver that is playing up again? Or—even more difficult—one that merely *might* be playing up again?

It was all very tricky. Besides, it was already gone six, and in not much over an hour Helen would have one of her delicious dinners ready for him—a three-course dinner, starting with soup. His wife had never bothered with soup unless there were visitors, and even then it was only out of a tin. Happening to mention this fact to Helen, quite casually, during one of their long, cosy talks about Beatrice's inadequacies, Martin had been amazed and delighted by the immediate and unprecedented consequences. Soup for starters, at every meal cooked by Helen, ever since. Home-made soup, too. Every Friday she would bring back great knobbly parcels of bones from the butcher and stew them up over the weekend to make the basis of a wonderful variety of luscious soups for every evening of the week. Lentil soup it would probably be tonight, with a delicate sprinkling of freshly-chopped mint. He'd noticed the lentils left to soak in a bowl first thing this morning. Clever girl!

"If my liver *did* play up—" the small insistent voice broke in upon his mouth-watering reverie "—if my liver did play up, would you come and ask me some more questions?"

Like hell he would! The interview was too long already, as well as practically useless. She only wanted to show off some more, buggering up the computer with her pretentious wisecracks.

"Well, no, Ruth, I'm afraid I can't do that," he said, dropping his outstretched hand at last and taking a step back from the bed. "I've got other interviews lined up, you see, (God, if only that were true!) and in this sort of work we have to keep to a very strict schedule. Otherwise . . ." He groped for some plausible get-out: "Otherwise . . . well . . . *bias*, you know. We have to be very careful to eliminate bias. . . ."

A non-sequitur if ever there was one: and lest she should catch him out over it (after all she *was* an ex-student of psychology, with at least a year or two's training in catching other psychologists out) he hurried on:

"So you see, Ruth, I'm very sorry, but I'm afraid I won't be seeing you any more. . . ."

Her head was pressed back hard against the pillows, black hair splayed out, and she continued to stare at him with her big green-flecked eyes, slightly bloodshot at the moment from the ordeal she had put her body through.

"Like to bet on it?" she challenged; and then, raising her voice slightly as he began to move away:

"Did you know, Prof, we're called the Pre-Morts here on this ward? Good, isn't it? 'Pre-Morts!' And down in the basement they have the Post-Morts! Maybe *that's* where we're going to meet next—had you thought of that? Like, if I was to have another go, tonight, and you were the last person to have talked to me? Asked me all these questions? You'd be in it then, Prof, up to the neck, right? It's a fifty-fifty chance you got, because fifty percent of us here *do* have a second go, and that's a statistic. Check it out if you want, but there's no need, Us Funnies know the score. Well, we should do, shouldn't we, seeing we're the fans . . . !"

Her laughter, clear as a child's, followed him the whole length of the ward, ceasing only when the heavy swing doors fell softly back into place behind him, sealing off the pre-morts and all their doomed concerns inside their proper enclosure, well away from the busy, important world outside.

CHAPTER 2

Martin backed out of the Visitors' car park, conscious, as he turned his head left and right, of the boyish lock of hair flopping to and fro against his forehead. There was a touch of grey in it now, but it still seemed to suit him, just as it had once suited the brilliant, rebellious student who still cowered somewhere inside him, immobilised by the lapse of time, and haunted for ever by an early promise that had somehow never been fulfilled.

An open scholarship to Oxford. A First in P.P.E., followed by a startlingly successful research year, and then, before he was twenty-two, a paper read to the prestigious Durkheim Society, and subsequently published as a leading article in their Annual Proceedings.

What had happened to it all? Where had the years gone, that he should find himself turned forty, and with nothing to show for it but a run-of-the-mill lectureship at a run-of-the-mill polytechnic? Where, now, was all that early promise, that arrogant, devil-may-care iconoclasm and drive?

He knew the answer to this one. It was right here inside him still, unused and undiminished. The question to be asked was not *where* it was—that was easy—but *when* it was that this early promise had begun to be of no use any more? Being promising had been his stock-in-trade as far back as he could remember; it was the thing he had lived by, had gloried in, and had so taken for granted that he had somehow never noticed the years chipping away at it, diminishing it, until, all unawares, he must have crossed that awful frontier in life where early promise has to be replaced by actual achievement. Only when his fortieth birthday loomed—quite suddenly, it had seemed, out of the clear dawn of youth—had it hit him, like a spear of poisonous light, that it is no good being "promising" at forty. You have to have *done* something.

By now, he should have landed a professorship somewhere. By now, he should have published a number of controversial articles in the learned journals, not to mention several books, both academic and popular. His name should be on the lips of colleagues and rivals everywhere—Martin Lockwood, the *enfant terrible* of Social Psychology, the irrepressible whizz-kid, the rebellious newcomer whose revolutionary views were setting the whole Establishment by the ears.

But he wasn't a newcomer any more. His views were revolutionary no longer. By now, whole books had been written about them, but not by him.

What had happened? Whose fault was it? It had to be *someone's*.

It was Beatrice's fault, of course. He should never have married her.

It was only since he'd known Helen that he'd fully realised how hopelessly inadequate a wife Beatrice had been to him, right from the beginning. Until then, he'd vaguely assumed that all women were like that—all wives, anyway—self-pitying, self-absorbed, bored by their husbands' careers, resentful to their colleagues, uncomprehending of their ambitions. It had taken Helen to show him how wrong he was—to teach him that a woman who is gloriously feminine and sweet can also be a tower of strength to man, a true helpmeet in trouble, and an efficient collaborator in the furthering of his career. All the things, in fact, which Beatrice had never been.

Not that Helen had ever pointed this out, in so many words, she was far too kind. She had never even hinted it. On the contrary, she had always gone out of her way to be nice about Beatrice, never allowing a word of criticism to pass her lips, and leaning over backwards to try and see her rival's point of view—even, sometimes, trying to persuade Martin to see it, too:

"Oh, *no*, darling, you know how Beatrice hates being alone in the evenings; I do think you should be getting back to her now." Or: "Look, darling, it's not quite fair to expect Beatrice to see it *our* way, when she comes from such a very conventional background."

That sort of thing. And the paradoxical thing was that it was just this unwavering generosity of Helen towards her rival that somehow, for Martin, highlighted his wife's defects to such an extent as to render them no longer endurable to him. Helen's tolerance, her lack of resentment, seemed somehow to set *him* free to be *more* intolerant, *more* resentful, than he had ever dreamed of being before. Safe in the ambience of his mistress's gentle wisdom, he could allow his own spirit to boil and splutter with such rage against his wife as he had never known was in him. And though Helen might chide him gently for these explosions, reminding him that "She can't help it, you know, darling," or "I'm sure she's doing her best, according to her lights," she somehow did it in such a way that he never felt that he had gone too far, or had put himself in the wrong by these tirades. Helen understood him as no one else had ever done; understood that the long-repressed disappointments and frustrations of his marriage had to be got out of his system somehow, and how better than by pouring them forth into a sympathetic ear such as hers?

And as if all this wasn't enough, she was proving herself a marvellous little housewife as well. Tonight, for instance, late though he was bound to be, there would be no fuss or recriminations; no "Where have you *been* all this time?" or "Well, don't blame *me* if it's all dried up!" No, there would be a delicious three-course meal done to perfection at whatever time he walked in; and candles on the table too, very likely, which she would light when she heard his key in the door.

What a woman to be driving back to through the February drizzle! What a lucky man, at long last, he was!

First, though, he must call in at home and pick up some shirts. Call in at 16, Hadley Gardens, that is—Helen hated him to use the word "home" for the house which, until the last few weeks, he had shared with Beatrice. He could understand Helen's objection, of course—it was flattering in its way —but all the same, it's difficult not to think of a place as "home" when you've lived there for nearly fourteen years.

It felt odd to be drawing up outside the familiar house in which he lived no longer; odd, too, to be inserting the same old key into the same old lock, just as if nothing had happened.

Inside, the house was in darkness. Automatically, his hand reached for the switch just inside the front door, and for a moment he stood blinking in the sudden light, waiting uneasily for his wife to pop out from somewhere. He could feel his body already braced against the encounter, whatever form it might take. Tears? Reproaches? A handful of bills?

"Beatrice!" he called up the dark stairs, after a few moments. "Where are you, Beet?"

This was another thing Helen didn't like, his addressing his estranged wife as "Beet," but what the hell, a man can't always be watching his step about everything, and anyway Helen wasn't here at the moment, was she?

"Beet!" he called again, louder, going to the foot of the stairs, "Beet, I'm here! I've come for my . . ." His voice trailed away among the echoes, and he knew now, for certain, that the house was empty. All the same, some kind of uneasy nagging of the spirit drove him to open first this door and then that, switching on the lights and noting, in each room, the blank, unlived-in look of a house in which a woman is suddenly alone, in a place much too big for her. He even peered down the cellar stairs, and tried the outside lavatory—though how she could have been there, with the back door securely bolted on the inside, top and bottom, he could not begin to imagine.

Where the hell *had* she got to? The sense of outrage that

was growing within him took him quite by surprise, and he stood for a moment in the chilly, white-lit kitchen trying to analyse the feeling. Why in the world should he care whether she was here or not? He'd only come to collect his things and go. In fact, it was better this way, the last thing he needed was another tearful scene. Or any more telephone messages from the solicitor, or to hear anything whatsoever about money. He was sick of hearing about money, of thinking about money, of getting letters about money . . . and above all he was sick of Beatrice moaning about money, her mouth pinched with grievance, her pale eyes red-rimmed under their sandy lashes, and her fists clenching and unclenching themselves as she sought desperately for some new way of hurting him. This was quite a problem for her now that he'd left home. The old ploys, such as burning his dinner black or refusing to go to bed with him were quite obsolete now that he had Helen.

All the same, and thankful though he was to avoid another of these scenes, Martin still felt obscurely affronted by the fact that Beatrice wasn't here to—well, not to *greet* him, that was ridiculous—but, well, to do, or be, *something*. To acknowledge his presence, even if only by refusing to speak to him. *Something*. It was his right, somehow.

Whistling to keep himself company, Martin set off up the stairs and entered the spare room, which for many months preceding his final departure had served him as bedroom as well as study. By his own request, most of his personal belongings had by now been stacked in this room ready for removal to Helen's; and now, standing at the door and contemplating his massed goods and chattels, he found himself once again gripped by an inexplicable sense of outrage.

Inexplicable, because he himself had ordained that this was where they were to be; had, indeed, transported several of the objects with his own hands from various parts of the house. Why, then, was the sight of them all here, all together, so infuriating?

Collecting them together in one place had been a *good* idea.
It had been *his* idea. How could he have guessed that his most
treasured possessions—his books, his filing cabinet, his hi-fi
equipment, even his brand-new dinner-jacket—would look, in
the mass, like the remnants of a church jumble sale?

Cardboard boxes bursting through their lids with bits and
pieces: piles of shoes, piles of sweaters, of pyjamas, of under-
wear—could he really ever have been the owner of all these
garments which Beatrice (at his behest) had sullenly un-
earthed from all the drawers and cupboards in the house?

And his expensive, ultra-modern reading-lamp, too. He'd
only bought it recently, and now here it was slumped drunk-
enly against some packing-cases, for all the world like a dere-
lict on the Embankment. And his pictures likewise, his framed
photographs of school and University cricket teams; there they
all were, bundled together, with string round them. Even his
new divan had been dismantled, the base upended against the
wall, and the sprung mattress lashed around with rope into a
great sullen roly-poly blocking out half the window.

It was awful. It was monstrous. Martin stood there almost in
a state of shock, as if he had come home and found the place
vandalised. And the fact that it had all come about in accordance with his own instructions alleviated the horror of it not
one whit.

"Beatrice!" he nearly screamed again, because *somebody*
must bloody do *something*: but of course it was useless. Bloody
Beatrice wasn't bloody here.

Past seven o'clock. Helen would have been expecting him for
quite a while now, and he was anxious, if possible, not to have
to mention to her this visit home—to 16, Hadley Gardens,
that is. Not that she would be anything other than sweet and
understanding about it, but all the same . . .

The shirts must be *somewhere*. Beatrice wouldn't have
washed them herself, of course, she'd have sent them to the
laundry, and so what he must look for was a slithery blue plas-

tic parcel with Sunfresh Laundry printed on it, and a bill for God-knew-how-much pinned on. Irritably, he began picking around among the clutter, shoving piles of clothing this way and that.

A door slammed downstairs. The front door it was, propelling a blast of cold air right through the house, and reverberating like a shot from a cannon. For a moment, Martin crouched immobile, like a criminal caught red-handed. Then, cautiously, he straightened up and tiptoed to the door. If it was Beatrice—and of course it was Beatrice, who else could it be?—then it was better that *he* should give *her* a shock by creeping down stairs than that she should give him one by creeping up. This would establish the correct order of precedence in the ensuing quarrel.

Well, of course there would be a quarrel. There always was. Trust Beatrice to think up *something*.

And now there came another sound. A laugh this time, a woman's laugh, loud and slightly mocking; and then, echoing it, Beatrice's pleased, tentative little giggle which meant that someone had just said something outrageous which she, Beatrice, would have loved to say if she'd dared.

Martin knew well enough who the someone must be; but for confirmation he crept across the landing and leaned over the banister.

The light was still on in the hall, just as he'd left it, and from his vantage point he could see the two hairdos from which flimsy headscarves, glistening with rain, had just been removed: Beatrice's threadbare perm, and the dark, shining up-pile edifice that belonged to Marjorie Pocock, Beatrice's evil genius from over the road. Not content with making life hell for her own husband, Marjorie was for ever in and out here, inciting Beatrice to make life hell for hers. . . . Martin watched the two heads move apart as coats were hung up, then swing close again as the pair made their way, still giggling, out into the kitchen. Through the open door, he could hear taps being turned on, a kettle being filled, the clink of crockery . . . the silent white-lit kitchen was coming alive now, for *them*. . . .

Footsteps. Little thuds and clatterings. More giggling. The scrape of a chair . . . the door of the fridge opening and then shutting . . . a low murmur of voices . . . and then a little shriek of merriment from Beatrice.

How dare she! For *him*, she had nothing but complaints and tears and ugly, whining recriminations; and now here she was screaming with merry laughter in the company of this interfering, mischief-making bitch!

Bitch! Both of them, bitches!

And what's more, he could guess who it was they were bitching about. *Him*.

CHAPTER 3

"Martin, darling, listen. This Ledbetter girl—the bit where she denies ever having been depressed. I'm just wondering—if you'd maybe probed a bit more at that point . . . ? I mean, we do know, don't we, that she *did* have treatment for depression, it's in her record. . . ."

Helen, from her seat at the typewriter, had swivelled round to face him, pushing her soft blonde hair back from her forehead in a familiar self-deprecating gesture: a gesture that seemed to say that the criticism she was voicing was merely a blonde, fluffy sort of criticism, unworthy of an important man's attention. When in fact it was nothing of the sort, but right on the ball.

"I don't know—perhaps I'm just being stupid?" she continued, knowing that she was not. "Perhaps I missed some of the preliminary data . . . ?"

She hadn't missed a thing, naturally. Martin, slumped at the breakfast table, still in his dressing-gown, still eating, felt at a hideous disadvantage. It was barely ten past eight, and here she was, fully dressed, lipstick in place, and all agog to finish the typing of this interview before she left for work. Her eagerness to be a help to him at this hour in the morning was terrifying, it absolutely made his stomach churn, but of course he couldn't say so because it was so marvellous of her to be doing it at all, fitting it in somehow before going off to her rather gruelling teaching job, at which she had to arrive on the dot of nine.

Reluctantly, Martin gulped down the dregs of his coffee and

raised his bleary eyes. He just couldn't think at this hour of the morning, the evenings were his time for thinking. Intelligent questions while he was still spreading marmalade on his last piece of toast simply made him feel ill. Why couldn't she be rushing round the flat looking for handbags and things, like other women?

"I don't mean," Helen continued, pushing her hair back yet again, and beginning to talk faster and faster, as if gathering speed for the running jump she was going to have to take over his morning lethargy. "I don't mean that there's *necessarily* any discrepancy. After all, a girl like that—a slightly unbalanced girl—might easily find herself denying, even in her own mind, that . . ."

Martin's early morning brain buzzed like a telephone that hasn't even been dialled yet. He could grasp just enough of what she was saying to feel sure that she was right, but beyond this his mind was a blank.

He decided to allow himself a little flare-up of petulance. Why not? After all, they'd been living together for over a month now, surely it didn't have to go *on* being so bloody idyllic? Not *all* the time?

"Just type what's there," he admonished her, repressively. "There's no need at this stage to start looking for discrepancies. Certainly not for the typist to start looking for them."

He was sorry the moment he'd said it; the quick dip and swing of her hair as she bent once more to her work told him he'd hurt her. He hadn't meant to, really he hadn't; but she shouldn't go on at him so.

To compensate for his momentary unkindness it was now necessary to go across and lean over her shoulder, to praise her —indeed over-praise her—for the excellence of her work, and to tell her how beautiful she'd been looking, sitting here at the typewriter so sweet and serious, and all for him.

She melted at once, of course, and he kissed her, smudging her lipstick so that it had to be done all over again. He knew how she gloried in this sort of thing: there can't be many history mistresses who have to re-do their lipstick *twice* before going in to their first lesson of the morning.

Twenty minutes later she was gone, and at the sound of the outer door closing behind her, such a wave of relief washed over him as stopped him in his tracks, absolutely appalled.

It was the awful familiarity of the feeling that frightened him most. This was precisely and exactly the way he'd always felt about doors slamming behind his wife. Any door, anywhere, ever. In her case, of course, it had been right and proper to feel like this; reassuring, in a way, a sign that the marriage was collapsing in just the way a marriage should collapse. Almost with nostalgia, he recalled those slamming doors of his former life, ushering in, as they did, stretches of wonderful peace and silence while Beatrice sobbed in the bedroom, sulked in the kitchen, or even merely refused to speak to him, passing him on the stairs with averted, swollen eyes. Whatever the form of her withdrawal, it was always an improvement on what had gone before, and brought with it a sense of release and freedom. No doubt the relief on these occasions was only the proverbial relief experienced by those who cease to bang their heads against brick walls, but all the same it was a welcome respite, and very understandable. What was *not* so understandable was how this very same relief could be experienced by one who no longer has a brick wall to bang his head against; who is, on the contrary, living a life as near to paradisal as mortal man can hope for. How could it be that the emotions engendered by a sour and hostile estranged wife could be thus transposed, in their entirety, on to the image of an adored and adoring mistress? How could such a thing be possible?

It couldn't, obviously. There must be some other explanation; and to Martin, with all his psychological training and know-how, the explanation was as obvious as it was reassuring.

What was happening, quite simply, was that his nervous system had, over the years with Beatrice, become conditioned to react like this to the sound of a slamming door, so that now, like any Pavlov dog, he was incapable of reacting in any other way.

Yes, that was it. A simple stimulus-response phenomenon, nothing to do with Helen herself or how much he loved her.

All was explained. His boundless and unqualified love for Helen was still intact. With a clear conscience, he could now permit himself to relax into this wonderful sense of solitude, of lightness, of restored well-being, knowing that it was spurious, a mere hangover from the unhappy past. He could make himself a fresh cup of coffee, too, exactly the way he liked it, instead of in that blasted percolator. Strong and black, and with lots of sugar, it would perhaps stir his torpid faculties just sufficiently to enable him to go to his desk and settle down to a morning's work on that God-awful thesis.

This was another somewhat disturbing thing that was happening to him—or, rather, wasn't happening. His thesis, which was to have been the turning-point in his career, simply wasn't progressing at all, or hardly. Already, the deadline was barely nine months away, and he'd scarcely completed even the introductory section; while his ideas for the succeeding chapters were still just as unformed—to be honest, just as derivative—as they'd been when he'd first prepared his synopsis. He had hoped—had, indeed, confidently assumed—that once he really got down to it his head would start humming with new and revolutionary ideas, just as it had done in his student days: that some novel and startling hypothesis would spring effortlessly into his mind, complete with inspired notions as to where and how to look for corroborative evidence. And once this had happened, he would then be able to forge ahead, recklessly outstripping that boring old synopsis, breaking new ground, confounding his critics, and blazoning his name in gold across the whole history of his subject.

But it wasn't happening. He'd been at it, on and off, for more than a year now, and not one single new or exciting idea had come to him. Every thought that entered his head had already been thought of by a dozen others; every avenue of research seemed to be blocked solid by hundreds of people who'd got there before him.

Inspiration was dead. His brain hummed not with new and exciting ideas but with an ever-deepening boredom and sense of defeat.

What had happened to him? What was going wrong?

The answer, at first, had seemed easy. It was the pressure of his routine work at the Polytechnic that was holding him back. Twelve hours' lecturing a week had been pushed on to him that year, despite his protests; and what with the preparation for these, and the seminars, and the tutorials, he seemed to have no time left for his own work at all. Also, as part and parcel of all this, there was the relentless persecution by his students, for ever handing in their assignments and expecting him to read them, or else not handing them in and expecting him to listen to their hard-luck stories of how this, that, and the other had prevented them finishing on time, and how none of it was their fault.

As if he cared. The fewer assignments the better, as far as he was concerned, and whether the omissions were due to laziness, stupidity, or their grandmother being dead, he couldn't care less, why bother *him* about it?

The whole thing was so pointless, anyway. There wasn't a thing he could teach them that they couldn't just as well look up in some book. What was the library for? It had cost half a million pounds, or something, to put up, and was supposed to be the pride and glory of the place: but would the students use it? They would not, not so long as they had the option of pestering him instead without moving out of their chairs. That's what he was paid for, being pestered by them, and the little beasts knew it. A Pestership, that's how it should have been listed, this job of his. . . .

Anyway, with all this stacked against him, and the best hours of his day devoured by administrative trivia, it had seemed plausible enough, at the time, to attribute his creative block to pressure of routine work.

But then, a few months ago, all these long-standing obstacles had been suddenly and almost miraculously removed by the granting of his long-awaited sabbatical—a whole year, on full pay, during which no teaching duties at all were to be required of him. Instead he was expected to concentrate full-time on what he had always longed to concentrate on—his writing and his research.

Hooray! A lucky break for Martin Lockwood at last!

But Martin's rejoicings were short-lived. No sooner had the distractions and obstacles imposed by his job been wholly removed, than a whole new lot of obstacles and distractions came swarming in, as if on cue, to take their place: it was as if there were a sort of Parkinson's Law of interruptions, from which no man can escape. What happened to Martin was that it was at just this juncture that his affair with Helen began building up to crisis point, and his marriage, long moribund, began to collapse completely. From then on, he didn't seem to have a minute to himself. Courting Helen, quarrelling with Beatrice: it was all incredibly time-consuming; and then, on top of all this, the actual mechanics of breaking up the marriage and moving in with Helen seemed to fall entirely on him. Neither of the ladies in the case would stir a finger to help him, Helen out of diffidence, Beatrice out of spite, but the net effect was the same in either case: namely, that it was left to him to cope single-handed with bloody everything, from making room for his belongings in Helen's flat to finding a solicitor for Beatrice, who was soggily doing absolutely nothing on her own behalf: just crying down the telephone, for which he was still paying, to all her awful friends.

Still, nothing lasts for ever, and by now most of the problems were just about solved. He'd accomplished the move to Helen's, had handled the terminal quarrels with his wife, and the rest was safely in the hands of the solicitors. There was nothing more to do. And so now here he was, his marriage at an end, his sabbatical in the bag, and ahead of him month after month of undisturbed tranquillity: long peaceful days of uninterrupted work in Helen's charming sitting-room, which had more or less become his study—followed by blissful evenings in her company, playing records, love-making, or working together on his thesis. The circumstances couldn't be more ideal, or more conducive to inspired and creative work.

And so what was going wrong? What was getting in the way *now?*

Because *something* was. Each morning, as soon as Helen was gone and he had the flat to himself, he would start the day by making this therapeutic cup of strong black coffee; and then he would sit, slowly sipping it, waiting, with decreasing hope, for some tiny spark of enthusiasm to penetrate his leaden mind and set him going again.

Sometimes, when there was a bit of Helen's typing still to check over, it wasn't so bad. It gave him an excuse, of a sort, for once more postponing the moment of creation. Greedily, he went over it line by line, taking a horrid pleasure in anything she'd done the least bit wrong. Altering her work, even if only by a comma, gave him the feeling that he was doing *something.*

This morning, thank goodness, was one of these not-so-bad mornings. There'd been the Ledbetter interview for her to finish, and also some tables about the incidence of depression in different age-groups. These she'd been copying for him out of a massive tome which ought to have been returned to the library days ago: and with a small lift of the spirit—because here was yet another little job which demanded of him no spark of creativity; in fact quite the reverse, because creativity in copying out statistics can lead to the worst kind of trouble—he set himself to check the accuracy of her copy.

Nothing wrong at all. Everything checked out exactly, in every detail, and Martin felt a guilty twinge of disap-

pointment. He could feel his mind, temporarily alerted by the
possibility of spotting an error committed by someone else,
growing dull once more.

Half past ten. Time for his next cup of coffee. By the time
he'd drunk this, looked out of the window at the streaks of
February rain, and tapped the barometer to reassure himself
that it was going to continue, and give him an excuse for staying indoors all day—by this time, it was after eleven. Soon, it
would be before twelve instead; and shortly after that, lunch-
time would be in sight, and the worst would be over. In the afternoons, for some reason, he usually felt better—so much better, sometimes, that he would even force himself out for a
short walk to clear his head. Occasionally, it actually worked,
and his head *was* cleared. When this happened, he would find
himself stepping out quite briskly on the homeward journey,
and with any luck would be sitting at his desk and actually getting something written before the brief spurt of energy began
to die. It was a sort of race against time: to walk just far
enough to get the mental vigour flowing, but not so far that it
was all gone again by the time he reached home.

It was a hit-and-miss business at best; and more and more
these days he found himself reluctant to expose himself to
these dreary perambulations with so uncertain a prospect of reward. It wasn't even as if there was anywhere pleasant to walk.
Helen's flat, pretty and elegant enough inside, was nevertheless
situated in a peculiarly dreary neighbourhood of tall converted
houses and ill-kept front-gardens. There was no park or recrea-
tion-ground for miles: from this point of view he'd been much
better off at home—at 16, Hadley Gardens, that is to say—and
so now, when Martin took himself out at all it was as a pris-
oner in the exercise-yard, grim and joyless, the sole purpose
being to prevent himself sinking into irreversible apathy, physical and mental.

While he ate his lunch—a double-decker cheese and bacon
sandwich—Martin kept a close watch on the square of grey
slanting rain framed by the window, fearful lest it should begin

to lighten, or the cosy patter of raindrops ease against the glass. Provided it kept on like this, as the barometer had promised it would, then there would be no question of the bloody walk. He might have a little sleep instead, and really get down to work after tea. Yes, that would be the best plan. After tea was always a good time, with Helen home, pottering companionably in the kitchen and tiptoeing in every now and then to see if he wanted anything.

A little flurry of rain against the window sounded like a tiny burst of applause: his decision seemed to be meeting approval even from the elements. Settling himself on the sofa, with his feet up, he closed his eyes.

And then the telephone rang.

CHAPTER 4

He took for granted it would be Helen. This was her hour—the school dinner-hour—for ringing him up to say she'd be home late. It was very unsettling, and it seemed to happen constantly: some wretched teacher being away with flu, or having to go to the dentist, the osteopath, the oculist—it sounded more like a nursing-home than a school, Martin would sometimes comment sourly. Or maybe the driver of the coach to and from the playing-fields hadn't turned up; or the headmistress was entertaining an important visitor; whatever it was, however unconnected with her actual duties, it always somehow seemed to involve Helen; to involve her, furthermore, in some task so inane that it was impossible to conceive why they wanted it done at all, let alone why they needed a First Class history graduate to accomplish it. Waiting behind for some child's father to turn up and take her to ballet class: sitting with someone else's form while they did their French homework: attending an emergency staff meeting to decide what to do about girls who came to school in slit skirts. Such trivia! Such drivelling, pettifogging nonsense! Sometimes Martin was furious on Helen's behalf, that they should so exploit her and misuse her talents; and sometimes, more disturbingly, he was ashamed of her for allowing it.

Anyway, what with one thing and another, Martin was relieved rather than disappointed when the voice down the phone turned out not to be Helen's at all. It was a male voice, vaguely familiar, and though he couldn't at first place it, he recognised immediately that it was the voice of somebody annoying. Somebody who had annoyed him before, who would continue annoying him in the future, and was certainly about to annoy him now.

"Lockwood here. Who's speaking?" he snapped, his voice already sharp with anticipatory irritation.

"Oh. Yes. It's me," came the idiotic reply; and immediately Martin recalled the idiotic face that belonged with it: round, cherubic, and adorned with a cheery, optimistic smile almost impossible to wipe off.

Walter. That's who it was. Walter Cummings, the pink, grotesquely contented Psychology student who'd been allotted to Martin as Research Assistant for this project of his. "Just to assist with the donkey-work," Martin's supervisor had told him, a little apologetically, "I'm afraid he's not really qualified yet to work on his own initiative."

Or to work at all, if it came to that. The donkey would in many ways have been preferable. Donkeys at least can't ring up in the middle of one's afternoon siesta to bray at length about their reasons for not doing whatever it is they are supposed to be doing.

"So you've decided to let me down over the Timberley interview," Martin barked, before Walter had managed to get any further than, "You see, the thing is, Mr. Lockwood . . ." "That's what it is, isn't it? Don't waste time explaining, let me guess. You're ratting-out again, as always. Because of the weather, no doubt," he added witheringly. "You're planning to upset our whole schedule because you don't like going out in the rain! You're scared of getting wet! You make me sick, you students, you're so feeble you don't know you're born . . . !"

Not in the least offended, Walter laughed the tolerant little laugh that he kept for his fuddy-duddy elders when they seemed to be getting themselves worked-up. If Martin could have smashed his idiot face in, here and now, by putting his fist through the phone, he would have done so.

"Oh, *no*, Mr. Lockwood, you've got me wrong, you positively have. It's not the rain—well, not in any direct sense, if you see what I mean. It's like this, Mr. Lockwood: what's happened, the little old bus won't seem to start this afternoon. It's the electrics again, I think, the wet's got into the electrics somehow. I mean, weather like this, it hasn't let up all day, has it, and the little old bus, she can't take it. It's not like she had a garage over her head, is it, she spends her nights on the streets does my little old bus, not like *your* swanky young . . ."

Martin gripped the receiver till his knuckles whitened. It was the ghastly, unshakable bonhomie of the little monster that maddened him most. Idle, irresponsible and incapable students were, of course, no novelty to Martin; but never before had he had to deal with one so sublimely unaware of his own worthlessness. Hidden away under Walter's plump, self-satisfied exterior lurked a plump, self-satisfied ego of terrifying dimensions; an ego so bloated with inner security as to be quite beyond the reach of ordinary reproofs and put-downs. Even two years in the Psychology Department had made no dent in it: Freud and Jung and all the other purveyors of guilt and self-doubt had simply bounced off it, like so many tennis-balls.

"Well, toodle-ooo, Mr. Lockwood," Walter concluded, quite unabashed; and as a crowning insult managed to hang up on Martin just before Martin had succeeded in slamming the phone down with such force as to set the little reptile's eardrums ringing. If only they'd still been there. And if reptiles do in fact have eardrums? Oh, what the hell! Damn, damn, damn!

So what to do now? Martin's first impulse was to get Walter's Director of Studies on the phone, and urge him to have the lad horse-whipped, or sent down, or something: but of course he could see for himself how useless it would be, in this present day and age. Nothing would happen to Walter, while on him, Martin, the whole thing would rebound with hideous force. Before the week was out, he'd find himself saddled with a reputation for being authoritarian, upper class, right wing, non-egalitarian and all that sort of thing. And then where would be his career prospects be?

Besides, even if, by some miracle, Walter's Director of Studies *did* pay any attention to the complaint, it still wouldn't solve the immediate problem. Satisfying though it might be to learn that Master Cummings was to be hanged at dawn and his head nailed up above the supermarket check-out, it still wouldn't get this Timberley woman interviewed as arranged, at three o'clock this afternoon.

He'd have to do it himself. That was the grim conclusion towards which everything pointed. There went his afternoon nap. There went his cosy tea with Helen, chatting about this and that. There, too, in all probability, went his evening session of work. His nerves would be in shreds after all this frustration and annoyance, on top of the effort of being compassionate and caring towards this damn Timberley woman. That was the trouble with depression. It might be a good subject to write about, but it was liable to land you with the most bloody awful interviewees. It could be like getting speech out of a hibernating tortoise.

Inwardly fuming, Martin flicked open the street-map and studied the route. Seven miles at least, right through the centre of town. Allowing for getting lost, and for traffic blocks, and for all the other obstacles that Fate so loves to scatter in the path of those who are already behind schedule, he ought to be starting just about right now.

Scribbling a note for Helen, warning her that he might be late—what a relief it was that she wasn't the sort of woman to make a fuss about it, as Beatrice would have done!—he collected his Timberley file, his notebook and his briefcase, and set out into the rain.

It was still raining quite heavily when he drew up outside the small, prim terrace house in which this Mrs. Timberley lived with her depression. He had already made some notes on the bare facts of her case—that she was fifty-four years old, married, and that the depression had grown upon her gradually over a number of years. He also had notes on the various drugs and treatments that had been tried out on her during this period, none of them apparently having halted by the smallest degree the relentless progress of her malady from "mild" to "moderate" to "severe." Over the years, she had had spells in hospitals, spells out of hospital, spells attending psychiatric out-patients. At the moment, she was out of hospital and "under Domiciliary Care," though who was doing the caring was not, from the notes, at all clear.

As he swooped across the wet pavement, shoulders hunched against the downpour, Martin experienced a small lifting of the spirit, akin to that of the hunter who has successfully cornered his prey, though it still has to be dispatched. At least he'd arrived at the damn place; the worst, in a way, was already over. With a faint feeling of accomplishment, he pressed the bell, and listened to the sweet chimes from within playing their quaint background music to this Mrs. Timberley's dark night of the soul.

CHAPTER 5

"Yes, Sir, pleased to meet you, Sir, won't you come in, Sir?" enthused the rosy-faced old man who opened the door to Martin. "Come along in out of the wet. Terrible, innit, this weather we been having? Still, mustn't grumble," he amended, as he helped Martin divest himself of his raincoat in the narrow passage. "Spring's around the corner, only a month away now, innit? That's what I been saying to my Magsy"—here he dropped his voice, and gestured significantly up the dark little stairway—"Perk up, me dear, I been saying, keep your pecker up, gel, Spring's only just around the corner! That's right, innit? Just around the corner. . . ."

So narrow was the passage-way, and so dark now that the front door was closed, that getting Martin's wet raincoat hung on a peg was quite a business, a sort of ill-choreographed little ballet, with the two men sidling around and across each other, trying to get out of one another's way; and all the while, Mr. Timberley—for this, presumably, was the elderly husband—kept up his flow of effusive and slightly servile welcome. "So good of you to come, Sir, so kind! My Magsy, she'll be that pleased to see you! My goodness, you should 'a' seen her, she's been that excited all morning, there's been no holding her! And now, Sir, if you'll just step up this way . . . ?"

The upstairs room into which Martin was ushered was small and dark, and very hot. A two-bar electric fire glared and hummed among the shadows, and there must have been some kind of central heating on as well, so completely had the wintry outside temperature been cancelled out and obliterated.

The windows, small and meanly-proportioned in the first place, were so cluttered up with lace curtains, net curtains, and heavily-draped velvet curtains that only dim vestiges of the damp grey daylight were able to penetrate the room, and at first Martin found it quite difficult to locate his subject.

". . . that excited all morning, there's been no holding her!" Mr. Timberley had informed him fondly; and Martin peered around the small room, stuffed with furniture and dusty ornaments, trying to accustom his eyes to the dimness.

Then he saw her. Lolling like a great cushion in a high-backed easy-chair, she had made no move to greet him; but she wasn't asleep, either. He found himself staring into a grey, swollen face from which a pair of tiny, unblinking eyes stared back malevolently. Or seemed to do so. It was impossible, really, to guess whether this unnerving fixity of gaze betokened active hostility, or merely an indifference to his presence so total as to be quite scarey; a relic of the primeval void before Creation was begun, and darkness was upon the face of the earth.

"Mild," "Moderate," or "Severe?" Tilting his recordcard towards the cracks of light from the window, Martin checked the category.

"Severe." Yes. They could say that again. He gritted his teeth, preparing for the ordeal. Ugh!

Still, here he was. It had taken nearly an hour to get here, and even if all the answers turned out to be mumblings and "don't knows," it would still count as an interview for his series. Well, sort of. He damn well intended to count it, anyway: social researchers thirty interviews behind schedule can't be choosers.

With the effort of a removal-man shifting a piano, he summoned up his bedside manner, and turned, all teeth and smiles, to his subject.

"Well, good afternoon, Mrs. Timberley!" he began, in that bright, slightly over-loud voice which always seems so appropriate in addressing people a lot less fortunate than oneself:

"How are you today? Feeling a bit better, eh? That's fine, that's just fine! Now, I wonder if you'd mind . . . ?"

Still the eyes stared into his, expressionlessly—unless maybe it was with hatred, who could tell?—and Martin found his technique floundering. But he was into it now, there was no turning back, especially with the doting, anxious husband hovering over him, tense with hope, waiting for something to happen, like a child at the Zoo. Martin pulled himself together. Averting his eyes, and fastening them on the comforting familiarity of his notebook, he proceeded with his formula:

". . . if you wouldn't mind answering just a few questions? Now, first of all, if you don't mind telling me, how long have you been feeling—well—like this? Kind of low-spirited, I mean? Not too happy? How long, roughly?"

Still the baleful eyes watched him, narrow with idiocy and the mindless wariness of dark forests, long ago. He sat, biro poised, expecting, almost, some ancient pre-hominid language to come jerking from her lips, all labials and gutturals, no T's or D's at all. She still did not stir, but a trace of spittle appeared at the corners of her mouth, as if she might be licking the insides of her lips; and at this sign of some sort of life, the old husband's face lit up as if he was watching the sun itself rising in all its glory.

"That's it, Magsy girl!" he cried. "That's my Magsy! Din' I tell you, Sir, how she's perk up once she got talking to you! Now, come on, me darling, tell the gentleman! He wants to know how long you bin poorly. Ten years, innit? Ten years come Christmas, that's about the size of it, innit?" He turned to Martin: "She's a bit nervous, you see, just a bit nervous. We don't have that many people come and visit us these days, not that many we don't, and so she's a bit nervous, just at first. Just keep talking to her, Sir, will you? She'll soon get used to you, won't you, Magsy, love, you'll soon get used to the gentleman." Then, to Martin, "You'll soon have her chattering away nineteen to the dozen, just you see. . . ."

By now, the old man was sitting on the arm of his wife's chair, his arm protectively around her humped shoulders.

"Ten years," he repeated, encouraging her, "Ten years, near enough, tell the gentleman, Magsy. . . ."

In default of any sign of life from his actual subject, Martin was getting all this down instead. It might come in useful somewhere—Attitude of Close Relatives, or something, you never knew—and at least it would pad out the interview to a decent length. He continued his questions, pretending as best he could to be addressing that lump of lard.

And how exactly, Mrs. Timberley, did the whole thing start? Did it come on gradually . . . ? Or was there some shock . . . ? A bereavement, perhaps . . . ? Some sort of family trouble . . . ?

Family trouble. That nearly always got them. Mr. Timberley's skinny behind fairly bounced up and down on its precarious perch as he chirruped excitedly to his spouse, cheering her on as if she'd been a football team.

"Come on, Magsy! That's the girl! That's my Magsy! *There's* a question for you, eh? Right up your street, eh, Magsy darling? She's got plenty she can tell you about *that*, Sir, and no mistake! Come on Mags, tell the gentleman! Tell him how it was that Christmas, eh, with both your Aunties here together, your Aunty Nell and your Aunty Vi, both here in the house together, my goodness, a proper to-do that was! Though mind you, Sir, I'm not saying a word against 'em, not either of 'em, we wouldn't, would we, Mags, God rest their souls. No, it was That Gwenda what started all the trouble. Wasn't it Mags? That Gwenda! It wouldn't none of it have happened, without she'd poked her nose in! All that fried food, too, it wasn't doing her no good. I told her at the time, I told her straight. Gwenda, I said, that fried food what you bring in, it's not doing her no good. Fried in cheap oil, too, you know the kind of stuff, Sir, cheap . . . nasty . . . wasn't it, Mags? Rancid, half the time. . . ."

There was a non-sequitur somewhere: maybe it would sort itself out when he went through his notes properly. Not that it mattered. "Breakdown of Extended Family Network" was obviously the category, and whether the story ended in Aunty Nell and Aunty Vi leaving all their money to That Gwenda, or merely with the more long-drawnout drama of nervous breakdowns, Valium all round, and nobody speaking to anybody else ever again, really, it didn't make a blind bit of difference.

Besides, there were all these other questions to be worked through somehow; he didn't want to be here all night. And so, as quickly as was compatible (just) with common politeness, he hurried the old man through this section, on to the next one, until he got to the last and (in this case) most bizarre question of all:

"I wonder, Mrs. Timberley, if you could give me some idea of how you mostly spend your time? Any hobbies . . . ? Any special interests . . . ?" In order even to enunciate so grotesquely inappropriate a question, Martin had to avert his eyes as he continued: "What, actually, do you do all day?"

The small eyes did not even blink in their piggy sockets, and once again it was left to the old man, still frantic to display his treasure at her best, to launch into a reply.

"Do? Why, my goodness, we're busy as bees, aren't we, Magsy? On the go all the time, you could say . . . Oh, you know . . . meals and that. And then it takes her a bit of time to get dressed of a morning, don't it, Magsy, these days? She likes to take a bit of trouble, you know, to look nice, make the best of herself, like all the ladies do . . . ha ha . . . they're all the same, aren't they Sir, when it comes to prettying themselves up, and we wouldn't have them different, would we?" He laughed again, happily, thinking, perhaps, of his Magsy looking her best. "And then there's lunch, of course: we get our bit of lunch, and then clearing it away and that . . . one thing and another. Do we get out a lot? Well, of course, it's winter just now, isn't it Sir, and winter's never been my Magsy's best time, has it, me darling? Well, it isn't anyone's best time is it, not when you think about it. Yes, well, we do stay indoors a good bit winter time, and that's the truth. But come the summer, my goodness, we'll be all over the place! You should just see us . . . out and about . . . here, there and everywhere, aren't we, Magsy! She really brightens up, come the summer, does my Magsy! Well, don't we all? It's only natural . . ."

Outside, dusk was falling, and by the time the interview was nearing its end, Martin could scarcely see what he was writing. Still, he persevered. There were some good quotes here, authentic lower class stuff, and this always made a favourable impression on the examiners. He listened patiently, anxious to get the ill-educated, cliché-ridden turns of phrase exactly right.

At last it was all over, and he prepared to take his leave. His formal "Thank you's" as he put away his papers and got to his feet were quite drowned-out by Mr. Timberley's rival expressions of gratitude, effusive and irrepressible:

"Oh, but it's been such a pleasure, Sir, I can't tell you! Such a very great pleasure, wasn't it, Magsy? You've really enjoyed it, haven't you, love? She's really enjoyed it, Sir, chatting with you like this. . . . It's not often she gets the chance of a real good chat, is it me darling? Somehow, people don't seem to chat with her like they used to do. . . . Still mustn't grumble. Anyhows, Sir, it's been a real treat for her, this afternoon, hasn't it, Magsy? She's got a lot off her chest, talking like this, heart to heart, you might say, it's helped a lot, hasn't it, dear? All her worries, all what she's been bottling-up all this time. . . . Bringing them out into the open, like, it's done her a power of good, hasn't it, Magsy? So come on, me darling, say goodbye to the gentleman nicely, and thank him for coming. If you just step a little nearer, Sir . . . just a little bit . . . that's right . . . she'll shake hands with you, won't you Magsy . . . ?"

The thought of taking one of those grey, motionless hands into his own filled Martin with horror. He could imagine the damp limpness of it against his palm. It reminded him of that awful party game they'd played as children, all sitting round in a circle, in the dark, while some unknown horrible thing—a raw sausage, perhaps, or a cold poached egg—was passed from hand to hand, while a voice out of the darkness intoned some appropriately horrific and well-timed story about severed fingers and dead men's eyeballs. . . .

With a small gulp of uncontrollable revulsion, Martin edged backwards, evading the ordeal with grunts and mumblings of apology, all the while sidling towards the door. At last he was through it, and out on the landing, now pitch dark.

"Mind out, Sir! Mind out for them stairs!" Mr. Timberley, close on his heels, switched on the light in the nick of time to reveal the short steep flight of steps only a few inches ahead.

And at that exact moment, there came from the room behind them a thin, exultant shriek; and then another, and another, so shrill, so empty of meaning that it was unlike any human voice that Martin had ever heard. He whirled round, sick with shock and incredulity, to stare back into the room, now flooded with light.

The slumped creature in the chair had not stirred. She lolled there, exactly as before, eyes fixed and vacant, responding by not so much as a flicker to the sudden blaze of light.

But other eyes had responded; unnoticed, hitherto, in the dim clutter of the room.

"Tweetie! Who's a good boy, then?" cooed the old man to the budgerigar which, from its cage by the window, screeched again in its joy in the sudden coming of the light.

"Tweet! Tweet!" it yelled; and "Tweetie! Tweetie!" the old man chortled in reply. Thus the conversation between man and bird continued joyously, while the great sagging doll lay motionless in its chair, and Martin, all the science drained out of him, thundered down the stairs, his feet stumbling and clattering on the narrow, awkward treads.

CHAPTER 6

Helen saw the note as soon as she came in, before she'd even dumped her two laden shopping bags on the kitchen table. As Martin had surmised, she wasn't offended or put-out in the least; though this ready acquiescence could have been due less to her tolerant nature than to her aching back. With a sigh of sheer physical relief, she sank down into the nearest easy-chair, allowing her carrier bags to spill out on to the floor on either side, revelling, briefly, in the fact that she could now go on looking a mess for a bit, and it wouldn't matter. Could just sit here, untidy, sagging, past thirty, boring, her hair uncombed, her tights laddered and her face smudgy with tiredness, and in need of fresh make-up.

The sense of reprieve was amazing. Her very limbs drank in the restfulness of it. For this brief, unexpected interlude, she needed neither to teach her class nor to fascinate her lover, she was off-duty, though for how long, of course, she did not know, and the uncertainty made it all a little less relaxing.

She looked at Martin's note again,

"Sorry, had to dash out, may be late.

Love, M."

Followed by a row of "X's," hurried kisses, all he had time to scribble before racing out of the flat on whatever errand it might be.

Late for what? Tea? Or dinner? If the latter, then she could afford to stay slumped here a little longer. On the other hand, there was no certainty about it, he might be in quite soon. Any minute, in fact. She ought, really, to be rushing round already, changing into her red wool dress with the gold belt, fishing out some unladdered tights, splashing her face with cold water, re-applying her lipstick—a softer shade for the evening. Martin always liked her to look soft and fragile after her tough and gruelling day at school. She should comb her damp, wind-blown hair back into shape, too, into a soft shining curtain, brushed slightly to one side so that her left check was half obscured. It was a style which emphasised her good bone-structure. Her profile, etched against the heavy sweep of blonde hair, looked almost filmstar-ish at times, and Martin adored it.

Beatrice had one of those blobbish faces, no bone-structure at all. No make-up, either, most of the time. She'd "let herself go," as wives do, and Helen, as mistresses do, was resolved that this, at least, would never happen to *her*. However much time it took, however tired she might be, Martin was always to see her well-groomed and at her very best.

However tired she might be. . . . Helen made a movement to rise, and then, overcome by temptation, sank back against the cushions. Just for a few more minutes. Surely he wouldn't be back *this* early, else why bother to write the note at all?

Such bliss to be lounging here, ugly, lazy, empty-headed, nobody's employee, nobody's ideal companion or perfect sex-partner. Just dull and ordinary. Helen felt dullness and ordinariness flowing through all her limbs like a benison, like an answer to prayer. . . .

Not to any prayer of hers, of course. *Her* prayers had always been quite other than this, and as it happened had all of them, miraculously, been fulfilled. To fall in love: that's what she'd prayed for during her teens and early twenties. And then, a little later, she had found herself praying more and more often that this time it should *last*: that there should be an end, somewhere, to all these new beginnings. And later still, finding herself turned thirty and still single, she had prayed her last and most passionate prayer: that her next bloke, whoever he was and whatever he might be like, should actually want to *marry* her, or at least set up house with her.

Oh, and that he shouldn't be too *young*, as so many of them were beginning to be these days.

And it all happened, exactly as in the fairy-tales. Her next bloke had been Martin Lockwood, forty-ish, and wanting to marry her terribly, right from the start. He couldn't, of course, because of Beatrice, but this made scarcely a dent in the fairy-tale quality of her good fortune. A man who can't marry you because of his wife is a very different proposition from one who simply doesn't want to, as any sensible girl can immediately perceive.

All her prayers, then, had been answered, even the back-dated ones about falling in love. She had met him at an end-of-term school party last summer, and had naturally assumed at first that he was a father of one of the girls, as attractive males of the right sort of age practically always were. She had noticed him straight away, a tall, anxious-looking man, with a lock of lightish hair flopping boyishly over his forehead, and his eyes fixed warily on a plate of jam tarts that someone had thrust into his hand and then left him with, ruthlessly, without further instructions. He had no idea what to do with them, you could see; he was the sort of man to whom a party is a drinks party, with perhaps a few cashew nuts thrown in, but certainly nothing as crude as jam tarts. He looked helpless beyond measure, and worried to death, like a Martian in a launderette—this was, in fact, the very first remark she made to him when he asked her, somewhat testily, what she was giggling at? He laughed then, and she laughed too, and apologised, and had gone on to sort out the jam tart problem for him in about three seconds flat. After that, he'd fetched her a gin and tonic, and while she stood sipping it, and listening to what turned out to be only the very first instalment of his troubles, she knew already that she was in love. *Really* in love. For the first time in years.

Beatrice, of course was the problem; and at first Helen had felt really guilty and unhappy about her. She knew her slightly, because she'd been at the party too, and they'd been introduced, though not by Martin. Helen's recollection of her was of a dim, rabbitty little woman with dried-out hair, a scuttling walk and peering, restless eyes, never still, never looking anyone full in the face, never settling on any object for more than a second. Later, she was to learn that Beatrice was short-sighted, and too vain to wear her singularly unbecoming granny-glasses on social occasions, and so all she'd been doing was trying to recognise the shadowy tree-trunk things that loomed up and spoke to her, Helen among them; but at the time the impression had been one of an exhausting and non-stop restlessness of spirit. It was no wonder that poor Martin looked so anxious and bothered most of the time. Anyone would.

She continued, though, to feel guilty about Beatrice for some time, even after Martin had described to her at length, and repeatedly—sometimes over long, lingering meals, and sometimes in bed—his wife's multifarious failings and deficiencies. Possessive . . . lazy . . . boring . . . sluttish . . . no good at cooking . . . no good in bed . . . it all added up to as leaveable a wife as any Other Woman could hope to encounter. And yet still Helen felt uneasy. She kept picturing the poor little rabbitty thing scuttling hopelessly about her messy home, picking things up, putting them down in the wrong place, pushing dust around, trying her best, in her muddly way, to run a home worthy of this incredibly glorious husband of hers.

But no, Martin would insist, it wasn't like that at all. Beatrice *didn't* try. If she had, things might have been different; but she'd never tried. Okay, so a woman can be a hopeless cook; but surely there is no woman alive so hopeless that she cannot *sometimes* boil potatoes so that they are eatable? *Occasionally* fry sausages without burning them?

"And half the time she doesn't cook anything at all!" Martin would complain, "Not even a bloody frozen pizza from the supermarket! I come home, worn out by a ghastly day at the Poly, and there she'll be, slumped in an easy-chair, her hair a mess, her tights laddered, and hasn't even bothered to put away the groceries. . . ."

Helen leaped to her feet as if at a pistol-shot, gathered up her assorted purchases, and fled into the kitchen. Already, it was past five, and if they were to sit down to their meal at seven—which was what they'd decided on, so as to give Martin good long evenings for his work—then it must all be ready, actually, by twenty past six. In a low oven, and somehow not spoiling. This was so that they could have a long, leisurely session of drinks, or occasionally of love-making, before dinner, just as in the old days when Helen had been only the Other Woman and Martin had come to dinner at the flat only once a week. Oh, the yearnings, the frustrations, the agonies of those days! And how easy it had all been, compared with this! In those days, there had always been tomorrow for the clearing up, and yesterday for the preparation; it had been child's play, in these circumstances, to produce a delicious three-course meal effortlessly and without fuss.

Beatrice, of course, had always made an awful fuss, about even the simplest meal. This was one of the wonderful things about Helen, Martin used often to say, that she was able to produce such marvellous food with no fuss. She was incredible.

And incredible, naturally, she intended to stay, as would anyone in her position. With one eye on the clock, she set the oven to heat, spread out the cod fillets on a floured wooden board, fetched butter, lemon, fennel, fresh parsley, a sharp knife, and set to work. If the main dish could be in the oven by twenty to six, then at six she could turn the fillets, sprinkle a few drops of lemon juice on each—*real* lemon, of course— and then lower the gas to the merest bead so that it would still cook, but ever so gently, without losing any of the delicate flavour. There would be buttered carrots for a vegetable—she'd planned these for the colour contrast with the white fish—and a few mushrooms, fried lightly and added at the last minute. The soup, thank goodness, she'd made yesterday, real Italian minestrone, and it only needed warming up. She'd grated the cheese too, on the fine grater, before seven o'clock this morning, but she must find a moment for transferring it from its plastic saucer to the pretty little jade green bowl which would look so good alongside the carrots. . . .

Chopping parsley . . . slicing carrots lengthways . . . whipping cream to go on top of the apples baked in syrup and ginger . . . and all the time the hands of the electric clock pressed silently forward, and still she hadn't got her red wool dress on, or changed her tights; and supposing one of the links of her gold chain belt broke again as she put it on, and supposing that after all Martin turned out not to be late at all, but early, as not infrequently happened when he'd warned her he would be late. "Surprise, darling, surprise! I managed to get away before the end. . . ." and then the ecstatic hugging in the hallway, half of her soul clasped in his embrace, and the other half ranging the kitchen, antennae out for something burning, something boiling over, something Beatrice-like and awful. . . . It had never happened so far . . . it mustn't *ever* happen.

With a quick, expert glance round her kitchen, Helen assured herself that her pots and pans, like a class of well-disciplined children, were all doing exactly what they should be doing at this precise point in the timetable, and then she dashed into the bedroom to effect a lightning change. Until she tore it off, she had not noticed how damp her pleated school skirt had become during the journey home. It would need pressing before she wore it again. Oh hell! Oh never mind, never mind, her hair was the really urgent problem, just look at it, bashed lank and stringy by the February sleet, no time now to set it with rollers, she'd just have to push it into shape as best she could with fingers and comb. . . .

It was a photo-finish, just about: with Martin's key in the door exactly as Helen raced past the winning-post—emerged, that is, from the bedroom, smiling, relaxed and with every hair in place to welcome him.

CHAPTER 7

It had been a lovely dinner, one of Helen's best. The washing up had been done—Martin always helped with this, no one could call *him* a chauvinist pig, he could see that it was only fair when she worked all day—and now here he was, his domestic duties honourably fulfilled, and with a long, peaceful evening ahead in which to get on with his work. Evenings had always been his best time for working. He remembered vividly from his student days that surge of energy that would come over him at nightfall, as it comes to a cat, or a panther; and how the words would pour forth almost faster than he could get them down, far into the night. "Best first-year essay I've ever read, Martin." "A remarkable piece of work, Mr. Lockwood. I'd like to show it to the Professor. . . ."

That sort of thing. It seemed like yesterday. He waited, now, for it all to happen again. The circumstances were ideal; a good dinner inside him and a long, peaceful stretch of time ahead, safe from interruption.

Helen saw to this. For her, Martin's work sessions were sacrosanct, and evening after evening she would fend off neighbours, phone calls, relatives, canvassers, like a blonde and beautiful guard-dog, creating for him an atmosphere of peace and privacy such as he had longed for in vain ever since leaving university. Now at last, after all these frustrating years, he had a chance of really achieving something.

Martin stirred in his chair, restlessly: then bent to open the bottom drawer of the desk and extracted from it the file containing the provisional synopsis for his thesis. His supervisor, Dr. Frost, a pale, painstaking academic, humiliatingly much younger than himself, hadn't been too pleased with the synopsis at first reading, and Martin had had to go to great lengths to impress on him the provisional nature of the document, and had endeavoured to mask its intrinsic dullness and lack of originality by dropping vague hints of some startling new angle shortly to be adumbrated, and to be expounded in detail in the revised version.

So far, so good; but for several weeks now Dr. Frost had been politely indicating that it was high time that this startling new angle should be taking some kind of definite shape; that something, at least, should by now have been set down on paper indicating the direction of these new and original thoughts that were to be the *raison d'être* of the thesis.

"There's a lot of supplementary data that hasn't been fully analysed yet," Martin would temporise; or, "I've got to get a further control sample before I can make any positive assertions," but his supervisor was becoming understandably impatient.

"I'll get out the full revised synopsis by the end of the month," Martin had wildly promised only a fortnight ago; had, indeed, wildly pictured this actually happening, in the first flush of his triumphant move to Helen's, where everything was going to be perfect for ever. But now it almost *was* the end of the month, and the synopsis had not been revised by so much as a syllable. Unless you counted the changing of the spelling of "vigour" to "vigor," which he fancied looked a bit more—well—vigorous.

"Vigour." "Vigor." Better change it in the carbon as well. There! At least he'd done *something*.

He flipped through the typed pages. They looked good. Wide margins, clear headings and sub-headings, good spacing. A synopsis to be proud of. The only thing missing was a clear statement of what it was all about. The new, exciting idea that was to be the focal point of the whole thing, and was to put the name of Martin Lockwood well and thoroughly on the map, was still missing.

Why could he not think of any such idea? He'd always been able to in the past, without the smallest difficulty. No matter how hackneyed the subject—from "Death and Bereavement in the Extended Family Circle" to "Incest and Pre-Pubertal Sex in Three Mining Villages"—Martin Lockwood could always be counted on to come up with something fresh and provocative, such as that sex is on the decline north of Birmingham, or that extended families are only tolerable when frequent bereavements are the norm. Something like that. It didn't have to be true, or even likely; it just had to be startling, and backed up by one or two case-histories so remarkable and so atypical as to stick in the mind long after the unremarkable facts had faded into oblivion. It is the remarkable, not the unremarkable, that tends to get quoted, and anything once quoted begins automatically to take on a dim veneer of authenticity that is almost impossible to dispel.

All that was needed, then, was a remarkable idea. Even the germ of a remarkable idea. What had happened to him that nothing came into his mind at all? Absolutely nothing?

It had been so easy, once. How had he done it, in those days? Was it a trick, a sort of intellectual sleight-of-hand whose secret he had forgotten? A game of skill at which he had grown rusty? Or what?

Martin closed his eyes, and tried to recapture the exact sensations of being that brilliant student twenty years ago: to relive, inside his head, those magical intimations of approaching breakthrough, that sense of his brain beginning to stir and heave, with bubbles of thought beginning to rise in it, like marsh-gas, slowly at first, and then faster: thicker and thicker, faster and faster, until his whole skull was boiling and churning with novel and astonishing ideas, his heart thudding in his ears, his blood racing, his pen flying over the foolscap in a sort of madness of creation.

Why wasn't it happening now? Why? Why? What was
wrong with him that all this peace, all this perfection, all these
long, quiet uninterrupted hours, resulted in such a deadlock of
the soul?

Getting started. That was always the worst part. Even in the
good old days this had sometimes presented problems, he
recalled. The important thing was to take a piece of paper and
write *something*, and then, with any luck, your pen would
carry you on from there. Pulling a little pile of clean, new typing paper towards him, he wrote, almost at random, one of the
headings from his synopsis:

"VARIETIES OF ENDOGENOUS DEPRESSION: A
NEW SYNTHESIS" He underlined it neatly and carefully,
using a ruler, and then sat clutching his biro, waiting for it to
write something.

Through the wall, he could just hear Helen's typewriter, patiently tap-tapping away at the Timberley interview. He was
glad to hear her working on it, not because it was going to be
much use to him—the whole thing was a dead loss, really, a
complete waste of an afternoon—but because it meant that
she must have quite got over that funny mood she'd been in
before dinner.

He still couldn't understand it, not really. It had all blown
up so suddenly, and quite without warning. There they'd been,
drinking together, companionably, as they usually did before
dinner. Helen had been looking particularly beautiful, he
recalled, and he for his part had been feeling even more than
usually in need of a sympathetic ear after his nerve-racking afternoon, and so it wasn't long before he found himself launch-
ing into the story of the frightful Timberley interview and how
frustrating it had been. In the telling it became, somehow,
quite a funny story, what with the budgerigar and everything;
and looking to Helen to share his amusement, he was taken

aback to notice that she was not, after all, laughing with him, but on the contrary was very nearly crying.

"Oh, that *poor* old man!" she exclaimed. "How he must love her! Oh, Martin, how tragic! Whatever's going to happen to them? What are you going to do?"

Do? Martin was thunderstruck. What was there to do, apart from resolving not to waste any more valuable time on such a pair of senile crackpots? Patiently, he tried to explain to Helen that an interview in which the actual subject simply doesn't answer at all is really rather useless: it doesn't fit into the series anywhere. Though of course, he allowed, seeing her still looking stricken, it was intriguing in a way, of course it was, and no doubt a slot could be made for it somewhere, maybe in the section on Negative Family Attitudes. And so yes, he *did* want it typed, Oh yes, certainly he did: that would be awfully sweet of her.

And so the incident had passed off, and soon Helen had been all smiles again, flushing up with pleasure when he praised her cooking, which he was at pains to do.

So that was all right. It hadn't been a quarrel at all, really: just a misunderstanding, quickly resolved. And so it couldn't be that which was disturbing his concentration.

The soft, regular sound of the typewriter had ceased. She must have finished the Timberley interview. She would be putting the pages together now, separating out the carbons, and in a minute she would come tiptoeing in, laying the document wordlessly on his desk and tiptoeing out again, her whole being set on not interrupting his flow of thought or distracting him in the least degree.

Suddenly, and completely without warning, his nerves were a-quiver with irritation, and he longed for an interruption, a *proper* interruption such as Beatrice would have inflicted on him.

"Martin! Did you remember to ring up the heating people

this afternoon?" or, "Martin! You never fetched the stuff from
the launderette! Do you realise it closes at nine?"

"Oh, to hell with the heating people!" he could yell back.
"Ring them yourself if you're so bloody steamed-up about it!"
Or he could go storming off to the launderette, fetch the stuff,
hurl it on the kitchen floor, and return to his work refreshed,
newly-injured, his adrenalin flowing.

Nothing like this ever happened with Helen, or could ever
be imagined to happen. This, of course, was one of the wonderful things about her, one of the major reasons why he had
uprooted himself and actually come to live with her.

Peace, he'd thought. Peace at last, in a congenial supportive
environment in which his long-repressed creative faculties
would have a chance to flower once more.

The pin-men were back. Martin stared down at them, in anger
and dismay. He'd thought that once he was settled at Helen's,
secure and happy, they'd trouble him no more.

But he'd thought wrong. Beneath that impressive sub-title
about Endogenous Depression, they were already mustering,
dozens and dozens of them, dancing and doodling across the
clean, expensive paper just as they'd always done, arms stuck
out straight as hyphens and legs splayed out like upside-down
"Y's." No feet, usually. A lot of them didn't even have heads,
so idle must his right hand have been feeling, so disinclined for
the slightest bother or effort.

Hastily, Martin shuffled the defaced page out of sight beneath the pile. Any minute now, Helen would be in with that
damned Timberley interview, and even though she wouldn't
say a word to interrupt him, it would be impossible for her not
to notice the little brutes if they were still uppermost. Having
safely hidden them, he now set to work on a fresh piece of
paper to inscribe once more that Endogenous Depression heading, once again underlining it with painstaking precision. It
would merely look as if he'd finished one section and was just

about to embark on the next. No one could guess that he hadn't written a single sentence all evening.

It did cross his mind that this sort of thing had been a lot simpler in Beatrice's day. No need, with her, to hide the fact that he was stuck, because she hadn't cared a damn whether he was stuck or not: hadn't even understood the meaning of that unhappy state. Miserable though it had been to be married to a woman who shared no single one of his interests, and couldn't care less about his career, her indifference had nevertheless given him a certain freedom of which, at the time, he'd been totally unaware.

Freedom to be idle, bored, unsuccessful, in a rotten mood. Freedom to spend whole evenings doodling and daydreaming at his desk without the smallest risk of anyone looking in to enquire how he was getting on. Beatrice didn't care a damn how he was getting on. She would never even have noticed that he hadn't written a word all day, or given a second thought to the fact that sheet after sheet of expensive typing paper were covered with vacuous little intruders from his subconscious.

If it was indeed his subconscious that was responsible. Weren't subconsciouses supposed to be full of dark guilts and traumas, too terrible for the conscious mind to contemplate? And yet when you gave it its head, just look what it came up with! Matchstick manikins, without face or character, symbolising nothing. Trying to arouse in himself some twinge of Freudian guilt, he tried adding a penis to two or three of them; but it was no good. It didn't stir up any traumas. It just made them look like camera tripods.

The sounds through the wall were different now. Helen was pushing her chair back, putting the lid on her typewriter. Her light step crossed the passage, and now he could hear her in the kitchen, clitter-clattering softly with kettle and crockery.

Tea, perhaps? Or a nice frothy mug of cocoa, sugared exactly right? Whatever it was, he loved the sound of her preparing it, it made him feel cossetted and cared-for. With a warm feeling of anticipation, he began to clear a space on the desk for the mug, jug, glass, beaker, cup of whatever it might turn out to be.

Damn! *More* pin-men, on this second sheet! Angrily, he crumpled it up and flung it in the waste-paper basket. What a mercy he'd noticed, and in the nick of time, too! Any moment now, the drink would be ready and she'd be at his elbow.

"How's it going, darling?" she would murmur, lightly stroking his not-yet-thinning hair; and, "Fine," he'd answer. "Just fine."

Supposing, though, he were to answer "Bloody awful!", which was the truth? Why, at once she would be all sympathy, her whole soul would spring into helpfulness as at the touch of a switch.

"Shall I check your conversion tables?" she would offer eagerly, all the tiredness wiped from her face at the mere thought of it; or, "Shall I re-draw the 1968 graphs in accordance with the new base line? That might throw fresh light on . . ."

And so it might. She really *did* understand the problems he was wrestling with. Over the past months, ever since they had become lovers, she had read up the subject assiduously, and was able to make really useful suggestions. And further, in her determination to be as unlike Beatrice as it was possible for a human being to be, she had even worked her way through a manual on Teach Yourself Statistics, and was now in a position to take over some of the minor mathematical chores which are so tedious to a really creative mind such as Martin's. It was for his sake, too, that she'd been learning to touch-type, and had bought herself this portable typewriter.

To have the woman in his life taking this sort of trouble about him was something absolutely new to Martin. It was wonderful, it was heart-warming. There were times, too, when it made him feel like a rat in a trap.

CHAPTER 8

"Darling, are you asleep?"

"Mmmmm. Ye-es. I mean no. What's happened?"

"Because if you're not," Martin continued, his voice pitched low as becomes one who is resolved not to disturb his partner's rest, no matter how great his own need, "then a pot of tea might be nice, don't you think?"

This last remark was impossible for Helen to answer. Struggling up towards consciousness through layer after layer of utter peace and darkness, she had not yet reached the stage of being able to think. It had been well after midnight when they'd got to bed, and she'd sunk instantly into a sleep of absolute exhaustion. Waking up now was like recovering from being dead.

"Wha—What time is it?" she managed to mumble, her vocal cords scarcely obeying her, for all her faculties were still fighting every inch of the way in their yearning to sink back into oblivion.

"Three o'clock," Martin answered, in the martyred tones of one who has brought the time to three o'clock single-handed— as indeed he felt he had. "I've been awake the whole time," he added, trying to convey the experience of it. "I haven't slept a wink."

"Oh, darling, how awful for you!" Helen's mind and body were by now propelling themselves rapidly upward into consciousness, ready to meet whatever demands were to be made upon them by the man they loved. Tea was it, this time? Then tea it should be. She slipped out of bed and into her dressing-gown.

"I won't be a minute," she assured him soothingly, though in fact she would be several minutes, the electric kettle having conked out and the teapot still being full of yesterday's cold tea-leaves. "Would you like some biscuits as well?"

"If you like," Martin muttered, meaning "Yes, only I don't want to be the one who's being demanding," and buried his face in the pillow, an invalid, sick with insomnia, and entitled to be waited on by those who are not thus sick.

Helen, grovelling under the bed for her slippers, wondered, fleetingly, was it always like this? Did happiness *always* mean not getting enough sleep?

A most cursory survey of her own past experiences would seem to indicate that the answer was, indubitably, "Yes." When you were happy, you got home after midnight. When you were happy, you had to get up and wash your hair before breakfast, because there was no other time. When you were happy, you spent the early hours of the night making love, and very often the early hours of the morning too. At those periods of your life when you have a man to sleep with, you don't actually *sleep* much at all. This was something that no one ever told you, you had to find it out gradually, for yourself.

The old kettle shrieked in her ear, and she jumped. She'd got herself out into the kitchen almost unconsciously and now she'd more or less fallen asleep again, standing there.

With an effort of will, she pushed her relaxed muscles into appropriate action. Milk. Tea bags. Teapot. Rinse out the tea-leaves, swish it round with scalding water. Make the tea, set out the cups . . . it all seemed infinitely complicated. Should she set them out on the little light enamel tray with roses hand-painted on it, or should she use the great oblong wooden one, which was heavy and awkward to carry, but which balanced better on the bed? No matter how ready for his repast Martin might appear to be, propped up expectantly against the pillows, he would nevertheless always give one more almighty heave just as the tray was laid across his knees.

Tea-spoons. Sugar. Oh, and the biscuits. Peering into the tin, it seemed that only Oval Osbornes were left, what had happened to all the custard-creams? Or had she forgotten to buy any during that hurried lunch-hour dash round the supermarket?

A sudden, piercing din, stabbing straight into her brain, caused her to drop the tin with a clatter, broken biscuits everywhere. She stared around, wildly.

The telephone? The alarm clock? Was she after all still in bed, dreaming? Sometimes, when she was very much over-tired, she did have these dreams; humdrum, horribly realistic dreams of the alarm having gone off, of herself having leapt out of bed, put on dressing-gown and slippers exactly as in real life; of hurrying out to the kitchen, putting on the kettle, setting the table for breakfast, checking the contents of her brief case, sometimes, even, setting out to catch her bus—when suddenly the *real* alarm clock would *really* go off, and there she would be, still in bed, and with the whole thing to do again.

The piercing sound seared her eardrums a second time and almost simultaneously Martin's voice sounded from the bedroom, aggrieved, urgent:

"What the *hell* . . . ? Look, darling, you're out there, do for God's sake go and see . . ."

Of course. It was the front door bell. But who could it be, at this hour of the night?

Something awful must have happened. Her sister? One of her baby nephews? The police, breaking the news?

And if not a family tragedy, then a murderer? A rapist? And if the latter, should she scream for Martin to protect her, maybe getting himself knifed in the process? Or should she urge the rapist to get on with it quietly in the kitchen, leaving her lover safely out of it?

"Go *on*, darling! You can't expect me to go, I've got nothing on!" came the agonised plea from the bedroom, and thus urged, Helen stumbled to the front door, unhooked the chain, drew back the bolt, and turned the latch.

The girl confronting her was small and dark; rather pale, and apparently perfectly at ease. Without waiting for an invitation, she walked past Helen and straight through to the kitchen. There she turned, speaking casually over her shoulder, "You out of a mental home, or something?"

Helen stood speechless; and the girl continued: "I just wondered. I thought maybe paranoia? All those bolts and locks on your front door, I mean. And a *chain*, for God's sake! As *well* as the bolts! Who're you expecting to break in and bash you up?"

Annoyance helped Helen to recover her voice.

"I'm not expecting anyone to—well—anything! It's just—well, most people *do* bolt their doors at night, don't they? And as for the chain—well, it just happens it's there. It was there when I came. *I* didn't have it put in. . . ."

Why was she apologising to this total stranger, about a perfectly normal and ordinary precaution? "Most people lock up at night," she repeated, more firmly. "It's only common-sense. This is quite a rough neighbourhood, you know." And then, almost as an afterthought: "Who *are* you, anyway? Who did you want to see."

It occurred to her at this point that Martin had been keeping a remarkably low profile all this time. He'd had plenty of time during this bizarre conversation to get himself out of bed and into some kind of garment and come and help deal with the intruder. After all, it *might* have been a murderer, albeit a female one. Or a gang, come to that, of which this young woman was the spokesman. For all he knew, lying cosily in bed, the rest of the gang might right now be standing around the kitchen in silence, knives poised. . . . Hang it all, he might at least come and have a look! Show a little curiosity! Whatever it was, a little moral support wouldn't come amiss.

"Who did you want to see?" she repeated, turning back to her visitor, in some puzzlement. There was something vaguely familiar about the girl—her manner, something—though Helen could have sworn she'd never seen her before. The sharp, vivid little features, the heavy loops of unkempt hair, the large, wary, greenish eyes—it wasn't a face you'd forget.

"You haven't even told me your name yet," she pointed out, "And it's jolly late, you know, to be calling on people."

"Late? Oh, that's okay," the visitor assured her airily, "I'm not hung up on 'late' and 'early' and all that crap. It's all just Time, isn't it, and what's Time, anyway? Just one cross-section of eternity, or another one. What's the difference?"

"The difference to *me*," retorted Helen, "is that *I* have to get up and go to work in the morning. Perhaps you don't? So *please* get on and tell me what you want, and why you're here. Incidentally, you still haven't told me who you are."

The girl shrugged. "You haven't told me who *you* are, either, if it comes to that. Or why *you're* here. What are you doing in Martin's flat?"

"Hey, it's my flat!" Helen retorted indignantly. "And if it's Martin you wanted to see, why couldn't you have said so right away? I'll go and fetch him."

At the door she paused, still angry. "I don't promise he'll be too pleased, though. Being woken up like this in the middle of the night . . . !"

"He's not being woken up. Don't tell me lies. He's awake already, I saw his light go on. That's why I rang the bell."

So the silly girl must have been lurking about in the street all this time, watching the windows. An ex-girlfriend of Martin's presumably, still madly in love with him, and hell-bent on getting him back.

Helen could afford to smile. This wasn't the way to recapture a man like Martin, absolutely not. He couldn't stand scenes and dramas and hysterical pleadings, nothing turned him off faster. Whatever this girl's hold on him might once have been, she'd ditched it good and proper by tonight's carry-on.

"I'll fetch him at once," Helen offered readily. "Why don't you sit down? You and he can have a cup of tea together, I've only just made it, it's nice and hot. Oh, and let's switch on the fire as well, you must be frozen. . . ."

Helen couldn't but be aware that, as one Other Woman confronted by the other Other Woman, she was really behaving singularly well. With some complacency, she compared her own civilised hospitality with the kind of behaviour that might have been expected from Beatrice had an old flame of Martin's turned up at Hadley Gardens at three in the morning, demanding to see him. She pictured the tears, the accusations, the jealous scenes. . . . Really, Martin could count himself lucky that it was all happening to him now with Helen around, instead of a few weeks ago with Beatrice.

Could count himself lucky; but would he bother to? Would it even cross his mind to think of it at all? That was the trouble with these sterling but somewhat negative virtues such as not being jealous, not being possessive, not throwing hysterical scenes: by their very nature they tend to go unnoticed, the beneficiary merely assuming that *he* is the one who is perfect, and never does anything to upset you.

The bedside light was still on, just as she had left it, but Martin was now to all appearances sound asleep, sunk guilelessly into his pillows as if he had merely dropped off while waiting for his tea.

He hadn't though. From the bit of humped shoulder protruding from the blankets, Helen could see that he now had his pyjamas on. She had left him stark naked. So! All the while she'd been engaged in conversation with the pushy young visitor, *he* must have been sneaking around the bedroom in the half-dark, softly opening drawers, shutting them again, searching for the rarely-worn pyjamas; and then scrambling furtively back into bed again, all ready to be found innocently asleep, but nevertheless respectable, just in case the worst came to the worst and he was forced to *do* something.

Helen couldn't help smiling. Such a typical male cop-out, and somehow she loved him the more for it. All the same, he wasn't going to get away with it. Not this time.

None too gently, she shook her lover by the shoulder.

"Come on," she said, "It's no good shamming dead *this* time! It's you she wants. Yes, *now*. You've got to get up and cope. I've put her in the kitchen, I've done the hostess bit, and now it's over to you."

"Who? What? What are you talking about?" Martin's feigned puzzlement was as unconvincing as his feigned slumber. Helen felt quite sorry for him, he was so bad at this sort of thing.

"A girl. A human female. Something out of your past, catching up with you, I should think." Getting a grip on his elbow, half-laughing, Helen dragged him out of bed, pushed him into dressing-gown and slippers, and set him off loping uneasily towards the kitchen, clutching his rarely-worn pyjamas around him, and looking—unless he was a much better actor than he had hitherto shown himself—like a man genuinely at a loss.

Although Helen had always prided herself on being above such sordid emotions as jealousy, possessiveness and the like, she nevertheless found herself hanging around the doorway, just as Beatrice might have done, in hopes of hearing what happened when Martin first presented himself in the kitchen.

Because you never knew. Despite all his protestations of bewilderment, who could tell whether his first exclamation might not be "Darling, at last!" or something of the sort. Even the man himself rarely knows in advance whether or not he is going to say this kind of thing, so you can't really accuse him of real dishonesty.

Such, anyway, was Helen's philosophy, and staunchly would she have stood by it, had it been necessary. But it wasn't. On the contrary, the words that came to her through the half-open kitchen door would have been music to the ears of even the most possessive of mistresses or wives:

"Look, this is a bit much, you know!" Martin's voice was loud and aggrieved. "How the hell did you get here? Who gave you my address?"

Then the door was pushed to, and Helen could hear no more: but she did not need to. Softly, glowingly, she slid into bed, and lay there, waiting happily for Martin, having got rid of the unwelcome intruder, to slip thankfully in beside her, take her in his arms, and tell her all about it. She was determined to stay awake until this happened: indeed, she thought she *was* staying awake, but somehow the next thing she knew the alarm-clock was screeching in her ear, and it was morning.

What had happened during the intervening three or four hours, she had no idea, except that Martin was by now back in bed, solid and inert, sleeping like the dead; though how long he'd been there, of course, she could not tell.

CHAPTER 9

Despite the disturbances of the night, aggravating, so it might be supposed, her chronic shortage of sleep, Helen found herself unusually relaxed the next morning, and, for once, with time to spare before setting off to school. Martin was still sleeping— it had seemed a shame to wake him after his broken night— and so she had decided to go ahead and have breakfast by herself.

It was incredible, the difference it made. Even while she ate it, sitting at their usual little table with its blue and white check cloth, Helen already felt puzzled by the aura of leisure which had seemed to surround the whole operation. How could it be that making coffee and toast for one could take so *very* much less time than making it for two? And the cereal was even more puzzling. All she had to do in any case was to get the packet out of the cupboard and set it on the table: how was it that even this tiny chore seemed somehow so much easier and less complicated when Martin wasn't sitting there waiting for it?

It was amazing. Disconcerting, really: and the net result was that well before eight o'clock here she was, breakfast finished and cleared away, and not even any typing to do, because with Martin asleep she did not know what to be getting on with.

It was a shame, it really was. Usually, it was quite a feat of organisation to fit in the half-hour's typing that she had set herself as a regular task before going to work; and now here she was, at leisure for once, with the best part of an hour ahead of her, and nothing to do.

This was ridiculous. There must be *something.* Goodness knows, the work was behindhand enough already, without her missing out on her morning's stint of typing.

Back in the living-room, she went over to Martin's desk to see what he had been working on last night. If it was something new, then of course she must leave it, as inevitably there would be alterations and corrections still to come: but if, as she suspected, he'd merely been working on the revised version of the introduction, then there'd be plenty she could do.

The desk was in its usual muddle, but by now Helen knew well enough where to look for the current work-in-progress. It was always to the right of centre, on top of whatever else was piled there, and the pages were always in reverse order, just as he had tossed them, face upwards, as they came.

But this morning there seemed to be nothing. Just the same old piles of notes, of cuttings from learned journals, and off-prints of other people's articles. Some of it was even growing dusty where it lay, like the accumulated hoard of an old, old man working on his autobiography which will never see the light of day, but meanwhile serves well enough as occupational therapy for his declining years.

Helen jerked her thoughts to a standstill, horrified. How could she allow such an image to come into her mind? *She* was the one with faith in Martin's work, she had told him so repeatedly, right from the beginning. It was Beatrice, his wife, who had no faith in him, who mocked his ambitions, doubted his powers, and belittled his every effort to get somewhere in his career.

Martin had been very bitter about it.

"But you're too old!" had apparently been Beatrice's first re-action to the proposed PhD thesis; and when he had retaliated with a whole list of distinguished persons who had acquired their higher qualifications at advanced ages—including H. G. Wells at the age of seventy-five—she had laughed nastily.

"Conceited old fools!" she'd commented, adding, for good measure: "And anyway, you can't even keep up with your routine work, let alone taking on anything else! They're ringing up and complaining all the time that you're late with this and late with that and when are going to let them have the other? How you can imagine that you're capable of taking on anything extra . . . !"

And so on and so on. And then, when the sabbatical finally materialised and put paid to that line of argument, Beatrice had merely changed her ground.

"A 'sabbatical?' What's that when it's at home?" she'd demanded; and when, painstakingly, he'd explained it to her she'd gone quite white.

"You mean you'll be at home *all day?*" she'd shrieked. "Home for *lunch? Every day?* For a *year?* My God . . . !"

Or words to that effect. No wonder that Helen, hearing for the first time of this mean and despicable behaviour on the part of his wife, had fallen over herself to declare her total and unqualified faith in her lover, now and for ever.

"But *of course* you can do it, darling!" she remembered assuring him as they lay in the rumpled bed watching the evening sky change from green to violet, from violet to deepest purple through the square of her bedroom window. That had been in the days when they had still been very new-fledged lovers, meeting only once or twice a week, and when every word exchanged between them was charged with double, with triple significance because of the shortness of the time they had for talking at all. Thus it had almost the quality of a vow, this declaration of faith in his powers. "*Of course* you can do it, darling," she'd repeated, over and over; and, "*Of course* people can go on having new and original ideas after they're forty! Look at Newton! Look at Bertrand Russell! In fact, I remember reading somewhere that the human brain reaches its peak not in the late teens, as used to be believed, but somewhere between forty and fifty . . ." Helen was always reading things like that somewhere, and Martin was enchanted.

Anyway, with such a background of passionate assurances,

such a history of unswerving confidence, how was it possible for Helen, now, to retract even an iota of this absolute faith in her lover's abilities? It had been the bedrock of their relationship from the beginning: this it was that had marked her off from Beatrice even more surely than her beauty, her intelligence, her generosity. In her, Martin had found at last the woman he had always needed; the woman who believed in him, absolutely, and whose unwavering faith in him was going to carry him to undreamed-of heights of fame.

How can a faith carrying that sort of a load be allowed to waver? It can't. It mustn't. Tensely, nervously, Helen searched the desk top for signs that he had been getting on with something last night. Preferably something new and exciting, but at least *something*. Three hours he'd sat here, ostensibly working. What, actually, had he accomplished?

The faint, gnawing anxiety which had been growing in her of late took another lurch upward into full consciousness, and her search grew more desperate. She even began ransacking the desk drawers, well though she knew that Martin would never have put away in them anything that he was currently working on.

For Helen was no fool. In her heart, she knew, as well as Martin himself did, that something had gone wrong, that the thesis wasn't progressing as it should. He hadn't said so, and she hadn't asked him, but the signs were unmistakeable. In her role as typist-cum-research-assistant, Helen could not miss them, passionately though she might wish—even try—to do so. Discrepancies; ill-sustained arguments; even blatant self-contradictions were beginning to appear. And worse than any of these—which, after all, can be remedied once the motivation to do so is available—there was a sense of creeping inertia impossible to ignore; a feeling that the whole thing was coming to a standstill. More and more, the stuff he gave her to type consisted of revisions and re-writing of earlier drafts, or long and only marginally relevant quotations from other researchers. There were moments—and Helen tried not to dwell on them —when she wondered if he was losing his grip on the whole project? Mostly, she consoled herself with the thought that after all she only saw bits of the work, in piecemeal order, as and when Martin chose to hand them to her, and so really she was in no position to make judgements. But all the same, the uneasy feeling was growing in her, day by day, that somehow he was no longer getting anywhere; that the momentum had been lost. Or, even worse, had never been there at all . . . ?

She had learned not to dwell on such thoughts. The important thing was to keep going. This morning, for instance, she could at least be going over the interview she'd typed for him last night, checking it for minor errors. There were likely to be quite a number of these, for it had been a long interview, and Martin's shorthand had been at its irritable worst. She could always tell, by a first glance at his notebook, just how fed-up he'd been while conducting any given interview, and with the Timberleys he'd obviously been very fed up indeed, the squirls and pothooks becoming increasingly hard to decipher as his boredom level mounted.

"A dead loss," was the way he'd summed up the Timberley session; but Helen, in her heart, hadn't agreed with him. She'd found the account of this desperate old couple unbearably moving, and could scarcely endure the way Martin was telling it as a funny story, expecting her to laugh.

And, to her shame, laugh she had. How could she do otherwise, when they were sitting so cosily together, enjoying their drinks, and exchanging idle chatter about the day's doings? How could she bring herself to wreck the happy intimacy of the moment with what could only look like a holier-than-thou attitude towards the anecdote with which he was regaling her?

And so she had laughed: had felt ashamed of laughing, and then, almost immediately, had felt glad, because laughing together had always been one of the wonderful things between them, and there had been, somehow, less of it of late. This was an opportunity not to be missed.

There weren't that many errors in the Timberley script, now that she came to look at it by daylight, and this morning, when she was no longer tired, it was easy to correct them. Only one page had so many alterations as to need re-typing, and this she did, making sure to crumple up the faulty copy and toss it in the waste-paper basket. More than once, when she'd failed to do this, Martin had managed to mix up her fair copies with the discarded ones, and there'd been hell to pay.

She'd emptied the waste-paper basket only yesterday, and now it was nearly full again. So Martin *had* been working on something after all, albeit not to his own satisfaction. She leaned down, curious to see what it could be that he'd brought himself to discard. Usually, Martin hung on to unsatisfactory drafts like a squirrel, hating to see anything he'd worked on actually disappear, despite the extra clutter that this habit engendered in and around his desk.

At the sight of the pin-men, Helen felt her whole heart dissolving in love and tenderness. Poor darling, what a frightful evening he must have had! Writer's Block, that's what it was. She'd read somewhere that *all* great writers suffer from this at times, and so why not Martin? Maybe it was even a sign of greatness, that now and again you have to suffer and wrestle in this way with the birth-pangs of inspiration?

Five whole pages of them! When she came to the tripod-like penises, she almost laughed aloud, all her anxieties melting into amusement as she scanned the absurd little figures scampering across the page. They were sweet, it was a shame, really, to throw them away. It would have been fun to keep them, to laugh over them together at some later date, when this temporary Writers' Block was a thing of the past. But Martin kept too much as it was, she mustn't encourage him; and so, steeling herself, she stuffed the little creatures back into the

waste-paper basket, and carried them, with the rest of the rubbish, down the three flights of stairs to the dustbins.

It was still early, but already a thin streak of sunshine had
found its way between the buildings opposite and slanted
across the stretch of paving-stones that led to the dustbins. She
stood in it for a moment, balancing in its bright narrowness as
if on a narrow bridge, and drank in the feeling of winter coming to its end. There was time, this morning, for these odd moments of rare and precious idleness, and she would have sung
as she retraced her steps up the stairs if it hadn't been for the
risk of waking the not-yet-up people in the other flats. And
Martin too, of course. This was another thing about happiness;
you have to be watching it all the time, to make sure it's not
upsetting anyone.

CHAPTER 10

Even the bus was on time this morning, which is the sort of thing which happens when you are in no hurry and are feeling at peace with the world: mysteriously, the world responds in kind.

The bus was less crowded than usual, too, and by going up to the top deck Helen found a seat easily. This was good, because though her feet weren't aching yet, they would be before the school day was over, and not having to stand on the journey gave them a good start.

Contentedly, she sat looking out of the window, pleasantly conscious that she was aware of the passing scene. Normally, this didn't happen, because normally she was on the verge of being late every single morning, and therefore needed to concentrate all her attention on making the bus go faster.

Really! And she a qualified teacher, too! How could a brain like hers, which over the years had managed to pass all those exams, be incapable now of rejecting the patently absurd notion that by relaxing in her seat and quietly watching the winter streets roll by, she would be somehow delaying the bus on its journey, causing it to loiter at the bus stops, take on more passengers, get caught up in more traffic blocks, and generally fall behind schedule?

An I.Q. of 130 or so ought to protect you from this sort of thing, but for some reason it doesn't, and Helen had long ceased to fight herself over it. However, this didn't prevent her enjoying a respite from the obsession when opportunity arose, and it was lovely, this morning, *not* to have to push the whole packed vehicle from fare-stage to fare-stage by sheer will-power. She enjoyed her journey, looking down at the damp, shining pavements and the scurrying people as if they were brand-new, and had never been there before.

Today, she was going to be at school really early, as she always used to be, before her lover came to live with her and to fill up every cranny of her leisure time. This morning, for the first time in weeks, she would have time to sit around in the staff-room before prayers, as she always used to do, listening to the latest gossip; and contributing to it, too, in no small measure, from the inexhaustible store of things which, in those days, seemed to happen to her.

"We miss you, Helen," Wendy Parsons, a colleague from the Geography department, had reproached her recently. "It was much more fun when everything kept going wrong for you, and this Martin of yours kept not turning up, and not staying the night and things; and you asked us whether a man who lay in your bed phoning his wife in the middle of the night could really be properly in love with you? Remember? And all of us advising you whether to give him up or not? Ah, those were the days!"

"Not for me they weren't!" Helen had retorted, though she could not help joining in the laughter. "They were hell on earth! Give me *Now*, any day! I'm *happy* now, Wendy, can't you see that I am? Really happy, at last!"

At this Gillian Crane, the classics mistress, had looked up from her Cicero, and had shaken her neat grey head pityingly.

"But that's just what Wendy's complaining of, isn't it?" she commented. "You're living happily ever after before your time, Helen!" And of course everyone had laughed again, including Helen; and then the bell had gone, and that had been the end of it.

They hadn't meant it seriously, of course. They were only teasing her. They were her friends, and of course they were glad, in a general way, that she should be happy. But all the same, since her love affair had attained its happy ending, a barrier *had* been created, though of what, exactly, it consisted was difficult to say. Helen herself was aware of it, and at times it puzzled her. It cannot really be that happiness, in itself, necessarily cuts you off from ordinary human contact, that would be absurd. Happiness is not a disease, like leprosy. By rights, it should enhance, not impoverish, the other areas of your life.

Partly, of course, it was simply a matter of having so little time. Since her lover had come to live with her, Time had become Helen's Enemy No. 1, and the battle against this adversary never ceased, either at home or at school. Rushing out in the lunch hour to shop for food; crouching over exercise books all through her free periods so as not to have to take work home with her; struggling to keep up with her share of those little extra duties which fall to the lot of any teacher. What with one thing and another there was never a moment left for idle chatter these days: and even if there had been, what was there, now, to chatter about? We had a lovely evening, Martin and I; no, nothing special, we just made love, and washed up, and I helped him with his Correlation Tables. . . . What sort of entertainment is that for an audience conditioned to the excitement of the chase—*your* chase? You can't expect them to go on being astounded for ever about the size and splendour of your catch.

Never mind. All this was about to be remedied, at least for this particular morning. Not only would she be arriving at school good and early, but for the first time in weeks she had something new and amusing to tell them.

As she walked from the bus stop, she found herself rehearsing the little scene:

"Such an extraordinary thing happened to us last night!" she saw herself beginning; and once again, as in the old days, the faces would turn to her eagerly, expectantly, hungry for the next instalment of her once-exciting life. She felt like a television personality back on the air again in a popular series that for some reason was suspended.

After all this build-up, it was a little deflating to find no one in the staff-room but Mr. Maynard, the senior maths teacher. As always, he was deep in *The Times* crossword puzzle, and did not even look up when she came in. It was a bit of mystery why Mr. Maynard, a married man (*very* married, Wendy reported, and she didn't mean it as a compliment) should always arrive at school earlier than anyone else, and leave later. It could hardly be excessive devotion to his job that movitated him, as he seemed to spend an absolute minimum of time either teaching his pupils or correcting their work, and he never talked about them. Unlike the other teachers, he neither complained about the tiresome children nor discussed the prospects of the more able. When he wasn't doing crossword puzzles, he was usually reading some terribly technical manual on how to do something, like restoring old china.

If he had problems in his life (and his face, lined and haggard far beyond his forty-eight years, suggested that he had), he never spoke of them. He contributed nothing to the pool of staff-room gossip, and drew nothing from it. It wasn't expected of him. It wasn't his duty to have adventures as it was Helen's, and so for the most part he was left to brood in peace over his mysterious preoccupations.

Helen certainly wasn't going to waste her precious anecdote on so poor an audience as this, and so it wasn't until several of the others had arrived, including Wendy, clutching her loose-knit woollies about her and muttering about the school's heating system, that she launched into the story of last night's adventure. The arrival of the mysterious visitor in the small hours; her unwashed hair and insolent behaviour; and what Helen had deduced from it all about her being an old flame of Martin's.

"Though the funny thing is," she concluded, "I had this feeling that I'd met her before somewhere, though I know I can't have. I've never met any of Martin's ex-girlfriends. I don't know what it was—something in the way she talked, I think—all that missing out of auxiliary verbs, and ending every sentence with 'or something' . . ."

"Oh, they all do that these days," said Gillian Crane scornfully. "Haven't you noticed? Nobody under twenty-five can frame a sentence correctly any more: another couple of generations and there won't *be* any sentences—just grunts and gestures!"

"I expect that's why they're teaching computers to speak," Wendy suggested cheerfully. "So that language will still survive even after humans can't speak it any more. A sort of sacred relic, like Stonehenge, or the statues on Easter Island! No, but seriously, Helen, don't you think you were overdoing the broad-mindedness bit? I mean, not being jealous is all very well in its place, I couldn't approve more, but all the same I'm damn sure I wouldn't leave *my* old man canoodling in the kitchen with an ex-girlfriend at three in the morning while I just went to sleep!"

Perhaps you're not as short of sleep as I am, Helen reflected. Aloud she said: "They weren't canoodling. They were quarrelling. I told you."

Wendy raised her eyes to the ceiling, incredulous.

"Really, Helen! I've never heard anything so naïve! Be your age! Surely you've learned by now that quarrelling is the surest sign of . . ."

"Yes, Wendy's right, you know, Helen," someone else chipped in. "It was like that with me and George. It was only when he started shouting at me again that I could feel sure he'd given her up for good . . ."

They were loving it. This was the old Helen back with them, as if returned from the grave; and at break, two hours later, she found herself once again surrounded by a little knot of listeners, eager to make the most of her brief resurgence.

Their questions, though kindly meant, were not always easy to answer. No, he didn't say her name, I didn't ask him. No, of course we don't have secrets from each other, he just didn't happen to have mentioned her before, that's all. No, of course he would have, if she'd been important . . . Well, I could hardly ask him there and then, could I, with her standing there listening? And by the time she'd gone . . . No, I told you, he was asleep. Yes, he was still asleep when I left . . .

So why didn't you wake him, then? Oh, to hell with his broken night! What about *your* broken night? What about Women's Lib? "You're too soft with that man, Helen, I've always said so. Much too soft. You'll lose him that way."

Did you lose a man by not being Women's Libby enough with him? And if this was so, did it not make Women's Lib just one more ploy for getting and keeping your man, on a par with lipstick or hairspray?

Aloud, she said, "Well, I did keep going in and out of the bedroom, getting dressed and things. I wasn't specially trying not to wake him. I was surprised, actually, that he *didn't* wake up, he's usually a very light sleeper."

"It sounds as if Miss No-Auxiliary-Verbs must have dropped something in his tea," suggested Wendy cheerfully. "You know; Revenge. Jealousy. That sort of stuff. Was he breathing, Helen, when you left?"

They all laughed; and Helen, though laughing too, felt a sudden unexpected little twinge of anxiety. *Was* he all right? Wendy's light-hearted fantasy about a drug in his tea was all nonsense, of course, but all the same, it *was* unusual for Martin to sleep so soundly, and so late. Maybe it would be a good idea to telephone him just to make sure. There was just time to do it now, before her next lesson.

No answer. She let the telephone ring and ring, for more than a minute. It was impossible that it wouldn't wake him, shrieking on and on, right into his ear, from the little table by the bedside.

Of course, he might have gone out already, though it seemed most unlikely, in view of his habitual morning lethargy.

Vaguely anxious now, Helen went to her class, and it was not until lunch-time that she had a chance to telephone again. This time, to her relief, the receiver was picked up almost at once.

"Oh, darling, I was really getting quite worried," she began, her voice lifting with relief. "I tried to get you earlier, but—"

He'd hung up on her. Softly, deliberately, he'd replaced the receiver and cut her off without a word.

Or someone had.

CHAPTER 11

With eyes that would barely open, Martin looked at his watch. He hated waking up and finding that Helen had already left for work. He couldn't blame her, obviously, since it was already a quarter to ten, and he didn't blame her. He just hated it, that's all.

He had had an awful night, and he was feeling awful now. It had been five o'clock before he'd finally got rid of that wretched girl, and even then he'd had to pay the minicab himself, as well as ringing it up and everything. She wouldn't even do that for herself.

Lying in bed now, his head thick with sleep and his usual morning lethargy heavy upon him, he began trying to piece together something of last night's extraordinary events: what had been said, and by whom, and whose fault it all was. This last was something Martin always needed to know before he could get properly to grips with anything.

Partly (he had to admit) it was his fault. He should have been more on his guard. He might have known, from her irritating and totally useless interview, that this Ruth Ledbetter was going to be a pain in the neck if she could possibly work out some way of being so. She was the type. He'd met them before, these interview subjects who seemed to imagine that just because they'd bared their souls to you in answer to your questions, this somehow entitled them to plague the life out of you afterwards, as if you were their bloody therapist. Transference, that's what it was, he reflected, and experienced a flicker of self-satisfaction until he recollected that if trans-

ference was what they were after, then they should be paying
£15.00 an hour for it, the going rate; not demanding mini-
cabs, and cups of tea, not to mention a share of the whisky to
which boredom drove him as the night wore on.

How had she tracked him down, anyway? Who could have
given her his address? One of those damnfool busybodies at
the Clinic, no doubt, their claws into everybody's business, and
paid never to let well alone.

What, exactly, *had* she come for?—apart, of course, from
making a bloody nuisance of herself, which, for one of her tem-
perament, was doubtless a worth-while project in itself. As best
he could with his furred morning brain, Martin tried to gather
up his tattered recollections of last night's ordeal.

"Look, Prof, if the answer's No, say so," had been her opening words: or at least these were the words that first clearly
penetrated his consciousness. He had complied with alacrity,
saying "No!" loudly and clearly, and without getting bogged
down in time-consuming queries as to what the hell she was
talking about. Keep it simple, he'd thought. Whatever it is, say
No to it, and then there can't be any more fuss.

How wrong he'd been. Far from bringing her discourse to an
end, the simple little monosyllable had had the effect of trig-
gering off a positive fury of communication. She'd gone on for
hours, the incessant patter of sound sometimes loud and stac-
cato against his eardrums, sometimes faint and far away, like
distant bagpipes, according as he dozed, and woke, and dozed
again in the hard kitchen chair.

Of what she'd actually said, he remembered almost nothing,
partly because of falling asleep such a lot, and partly because
of being too annoyed to listen properly even when he was
awake. Annoyed not only with Ruth for landing herself on him
at this unearthly hour, but with Helen, too, for allowing it.
What the hell did she think she was doing, allowing her lover
to spend half the night closeted in the kitchen with a brazen
little hussy like this? And providing them with tea and biscuits
too, for God's sake! Why couldn't she be jealous and posses-

sive, like other women? Then maybe he, Martin, would have had a decent night's sleep, and wouldn't be feeling so absolutely frightful this morning.

Ten o'clock. Glumly, and with frightful effort, Martin dragged himself out of bed, and huddling into his dressing-gown padded out to the kitchen.

Last night's debris had been cleared away, and the breakfast table was neatly and invitingly laid for one. In a tiny glass jar beside his plate, Helen had placed two golden crocuses, the first of the season. She was saying it with flowers, saying something to the effect that even far away in her classroom, she was still loving him.

Or was still keeping an eye on him. That's more what it felt like, somehow. Saying it with flowers has always been a chancy business, the message sent often becoming sadly scrambled by the time it reaches the recipient. Martin felt trapped, and somehow put-upon by this all-embracing care and concern that never seemed to let up, day or night.

Impatiently, he pushed the flowers aside to make room for the coffee-pot, and then slowly, resentfully, and not very efficiently he set about making his own breakfast. This morning, perversely, he decided to have a boiled egg with his toast, a thing he rarely did: and a great nuisance it proved to be, what with finding the right pan, and timing it, and everything. It was a sort of retaliation for the flowers: just *look* at all the bothersome tasks you're leaving me to do all by myself.

The ringing of the telephone almost pitched him out of his chair. The shock was awful, he was filled with a nameless dread, which after a very few moments he was able to identify all too easily as the usual and familiar dread lest somebody was going to expect him to do something.

He just couldn't face it, not at this hour in the morning. He sat with his head in his hands waiting for it to stop.

That damn Ledbetter girl! Under the impact of the din, a flicker of memory was surfacing from his subconscious . . .

something she'd said . . . ? asked him about . . . ? catching him at a moment when he was too exhausted to argue . . . ? Yes, that was it. Something about phoning him. Phoning him this morning for his decision.

What decision? How people do keep on at you! Crouched at the table, shoulders hunched, head down, like a man under machine gun fire, Martin tried to make his mind a blank; and then, when this didn't work, he fell to counting the rings as they blared through the flat.

Surely it must stop *some* time? Has there ever been a case of a telephone that goes on ringing *for ever*? In the *Guinness Book of Records* would it be . . . ?

And at last, of course, it *did* stop. Quite shaken, Martin raised his head, and warily tried to resume his breakfast. By now his appetite was quite gone. The coffee was cold, the egg was hard, and a tight knot of rage, almost indistinguishable from heart-burn, was forming in his gullet. Why did people have to do this to him? Why couldn't they leave him alone?

At the sight of the little golden flowers, still beaming their innocent message at him as if nothing had happened, he almost choked.

It was all Helen's fault, somehow. He couldn't explain it or analyse it, but it was.

Work was impossible. Even leafing through his amended notes for Section II. The Aetiology of Depression in Middle Life, made him feel quite ill. There wasn't an idea anywhere that hadn't been cribbed from someone else, not a paragraph which wasn't heavy with platitudes and padding.

Endogenous Depression. Reactive Depression. Menopausal Depression. Early signs and symptoms. There wasn't a single thing here which wasn't common knowledge, elementary text-book stuff. How long could he keep up the delusion that these worn-out commonplaces were going to lead somehow to some brilliant new synthesis, some novel and startling hypothesis which would revolutionise the whole academic approach to the subject, and open up avenues of treatment yet undreamed?

"The typical onset is insidious," he had written, as if no one had ever noticed this before. "His early symptoms are commonly attributed by the patient to adverse factors in his environment. Guilt and self-blame may already be evident at this stage, blah blah blah, commonly projected on to those close to him, blah blah blah, resulting in progressive withdrawal from supportive relationships, blah blah blah . . ."

It was almost a relief when the front door bell sliced through this tired re-hash of entrenched platitudes. Deeply though Martin loathed all the kinds of people it could possibly be—meter-readers, neighbours, insurance salesmen, window-cleaners and the like—nevertheless, *any* distraction was better than none. Hating whoever it was would at least be a change from hating everything else.

A scowl on his face, and a faint, pleasurable stirring of adrenalin in his veins, Martin strode towards the door. There might even be an opportunity to be rude to somebody. You never knew.

Ruth Ledbetter sidled in like an experienced stray cat, giving him no chance to shut the door on her. Once inside, as stray cats will, she made straight for the electric fire with its two bars on.

"What a bloody waste," she remarked, bending down the better to warm her small, ungloved hands, mottled with cold. "*Two* bars! You a bloody millionaire, or something?"

"I'll turn them off if you like," Martin threatened, irritated by the blatant advantage she was taking of the condemned luxury; and almost instantly he realised what a mistake it was to have been thus side-tracked. He should have concentrated all his energies on telling her to *go*: to get out, to scram, to piss off. It was too late now. This sort of thing has to be said in the heat of the moment, across a still un-breached threshold, and with your hand still in the position of power on the doorhandle. You can't do it once the visitor has established a bridgehead within your territory, has already penetrated as far as the sitting-room, and is stepping, cat-like, around the perimeter of the carpet, examining every picture, every bit of decoration, with a sort of wondering contempt.

"Christ! It's a sort of tomb, isn't it?" was her first remark, "A sort of Do-it-Yourself mortuary."

Thunderstruck, Martin took two steps backwards and, half-expecting to find the room indeed changed, looked wildly about him.

It was a pretty room, he'd always thought so; even elegant, for Helen had excellent taste, though little money to spend. The white-painted bookshelves were sparkling, the carpet newly-vacuumed, and vases of autumn leaves and berries, still beautiful, stood here and there about the room, the muted colours reflected softly in polished wood and gleaming brass.

"Dead things!" Ruth pointed. "She keeps dead things to look at in the evenings! She tears them from the live trees and hedges, and brings them back here so she can watch them die! She a necrophiliac or something, your girlfriend?"

Martin was completely thrown. He could think of no words with which to reply to these bizarre and outrageous accusations. The sheer insolence of it left him speechless.

And yet, under his very proper sense of outrage, he was aware that he was feeling better than he had for months. The heavy mornings dullness that had plagued him for so long was suddenly quite gone. He felt a sort of glee, a secret inner gloating impossible to describe.

Something was happening at last.

CHAPTER 12

"No sex," said Ruth, sipping her coffee delicately through neat, pointed lips, like a small bird. "I hate sex. If you try to make me have sex, then it's all off, I won't help you at all."

Why couldn't she say "make love"? "Have sex" was such an ugly, harsh phrase, especially from so young a girl. Not that it mattered. Nothing was further from his mind at this particular juncture, and, as politely as he could, he told her so, adding: "I've got my own girlfriend, you know, here, living with me, and I love her very much."

"You do?" Ruth looked at him reflectively, with something of the air of a doctor who, having diagnosed a mortal disease, is uncertain just how much of the truth to reveal to the patient. "Then how come you're in a depression? A *clinical* depression," she amended, showing off, with childlike vanity, her familiarity with technical terms. "Listen!" She picked up a page of manuscript from his desk as if at random—though Martin felt quite sure that she'd been prying about among his papers while he'd been making the coffee—"Just listen to this!" and she proceeded to read his own words back at him, mimicking what she imagined to be the pompous tones of an authority on the subject:

"Among early symptoms, insomnia is frequently thé one that first brings the patient to his doctor's surgery . . .

She skimmed through the paragraph:

" 'Tiredness . . . Irritability . . . failure of concentration . . . loss of intellectual drive . . . impoverishment of affect . . . sense of failure . . . deterioration of personal relationships . . . exhaustion and lethargy, especially in the mornings . . . progressive slowing-up of thought-processes . . .'

"So who wants to read your autobiography, Prof? I thought this was meant to be a *thesis?*"

"It *is* a thesis!—" Martin was beginning indignantly, but she interrupted him:

"Autobiography," she insisted. "A walking case-history!" She sniggered, and tossed the page back among the others. "The case-history of a certain M 40 B, Social Psychology lecturer. Victim of Life Events Nos. 2, 5, 6 and 7. To wit: Broken Marriage, Change of Domicile, Acquisition of New Life Partner, Failure to Achieve Promotion at work. Adding up to a total of 470 points on the Life-Stress Scale. Friends: nil. Occupation: bloody nothing. No wonder he's depressed. Right?"

Martin shrugged. He wasn't going to let her see that her snap diagnosis had struck home. If it *was* a snap diagnosis? Some way or another, she seemed to have discovered one hell of a lot about him.

"You exaggerate," he said lightly. "Naturally, I'm aware that I have certain depressive tendencies, most academics have, but—"

"Not tendencies. A full-blown clinical depression," she insisted. "Endogenous." She loved using these polysyllables, you could tell. And she was using them correctly, damn her.

Abruptly, Martin changed the subject.

"You said you had a proposition to make to me," he suggested, taking her coffee cup rather pointedly away from her. She was irritating him almost past endurance by scooping out the sugary dregs with a teaspoon and then licking at them with her quick darting tongue. "Did you want some more?" He held the cup well away from her, inquiringly, and when she shook her head he put it down safely out of her reach. "Now, tell me, Ruth, exactly what it was you had in mind?"

"I told you last night," she said sulkily; and then, when he waited for her to continue, she added nastily: "That's another symptom of depression, you know; never listening to a word anybody says."

It was, too. He couldn't fault her on her textbook knowledge.

"It can also be a symptom of boredom," he pointed out drily. "And of prolonged sleep-deprivation. It's a syndrome you may encounter quite often if you make a habit of waking people up in the small-hours and forcing them to sit up all night while you tell the story of your life. It *was* the story of your life you were telling, I take it?"

Well, of course it was. They were all the same, these neurotic types. And now, just like the rest of them, she was sulking. Not looking at him. Not speaking. Fidgeting in the big chair. Was it for this that he'd shaken the dust of his student seminars off his feet for a whole year? So touchy, some of these girls, it made you wonder how they'd ever picked their way through their pampered lives even thus far.

At last, she spoke.

"You're looking at my legs," she accused, pulling her short navy skirt as far over her knees as it would go; and now, of course, he did look at them, for the first time. Skinny they were, white as peeled mushrooms under her laddered tights. Not attractive at all. He felt boredom, like the beginning of an illness, stirring restlessly in his vitals, and knew that he must act quickly before it got him.

"Look, Ruth, I'm sorry if I don't remember too well just what it was we were talking about last night, but it was bloody late, you know. If you want people to listen to you, you should pick a time convenient to them as well as to yourself."

It felt rather good, having a young person to patronise again. Perhaps he was missing his students more than he realised.

"However," he continued, pleased by his little homily, "it so happens that this *is* a time convenient to me, and so I'll be happy to give you a few minutes—" he glanced importantly at his watch, just as if the time it indicated made a blind bit of difference. "But do please get on with it, my dear. I haven't got all day."

He had, of course, but that was beside the point. The incipient boredom was beginning to gnaw, like an ulcer, inside him.

"Jumpy, aren't you?" she remarked, and stretching out her thin legs across the hearthrug, she leaned back in the chair and contemplated him, a small smile beginning to twitch at the corners of her lips. "It's a pity you couldn't be bothered to listen to me last night, Mr. Lockwood, because the proposition I put up to you then was quite something. It could have been all yours, Daddy-O. Like, you know, real neat.

"It's too late now, so that's Curtains for Proposition A. Which leaves us Proposition B. Right? Right, Mr. Lockwood?"

"Why—er—yes." Martin was somehow taken by surprise, he'd thought the sentence was going on for ages yet. "Yes. I suppose so. Yes. I mean 'Right,'" he amended, as if giving the correct password. "'Right.'"

"Right," she echoed, on a curious note of relief, as if the first small step of some complex and hazardous project had after all gone according to plan. "Right, Mr. Lockwood. Proposition B, then. A business proposition, plain and simple. Would you like me to do your interviews for you? Take them over, the whole lot, and finish them? I could. I'm experienced. And I happen to know you've got behind with them."

How did she happen to know? Who had told her? First his address, here at Helen's: and now this. He began to feel hunted down, closed in upon, by persons unknown.

He wasn't going to let her see his discomfiture.

"As a matter of fact, Ruth, you happen to be perfectly right," he said, with assumed nonchalance. "Though how you came to have access to confidential information of this nature, I really cannot . . ."

"Oh, Walter told me," she said easily; and then, misinterpreting Martin's startled look, she kindly explained: "You know. Walter Cummings. The guy who works for you. A big, fat goofy chap, as thick as two boards."

Martin had been about to express outrage at this casual exchange of confidential information among his subordinates, but now he thought better of it. He liked her description of Walter. A perceptive girl. Maybe she *would* make a good interviewer?

He thought about it, and the more he thought about it the more delectable seemed the prospect of getting help—competent, professional help, not Walter's reluctant and intermittent fumblings—with his frightful arrears of interviews. And not merely help; unless he had misunderstood her, she was proposing to take over the job completely, to do the whole lot of them herself, just like that. The very idea of it set his heart pounding with sheer, incredulous relief. To get the bloody things *done*, without having to bloody *do* them! It was like a dream come true.

If only it *did* come true? If only there wasn't some snag somewhere?

He looked at his prospective assistant thoughtfully: at the pale, sharp features, the bright, calculating eyes.

The hell with it! Of course she was calculating, and so, for that matter, was he: why else would he be looking her up and down like this, weighing up the advantages and possible disadvantages of employing her? Everyone calculates, applies the What's-in-it-for-me test to any new project. They'd be fools not to, and the last thing he wanted was another fool on the job.

Yes, he decided, she'd do. She had brains, she had determination, and above all she had the cheek of the devil, which, particularly in the case of depth-interviewing, is a qualification in itself.

"What are your qualifications?" he asked. He didn't want her to think it was a walkover, getting this job, though of course it was: at 80p an hour, how could it be otherwise? Nor did he want her to think he would take just anybody, though

of course he would, that's how he'd got Walter. But you don't
get that sort of bad luck twice in a lifetime, surely?

"Qualifications? Oh, well, of course I haven't got a degree or
any of that crap," she answered him, as if this was a recom-
mendation in itself. Which of course it was, in a way: a graduate would kick up no end of tedious fuss about the pay scale.
"Walter said it didn't matter," she continued. "He says he
hasn't got one, either."

Walter this. Walter that. Martin felt uneasy.

"A friend of yours, is he?" he asked cautiously. He was wary
of this sort of thing. He didn't want the two of them getting
together on the job, comparing notes, ganging up on him. It
could easily happen.

Her reply was reassuring.

"What, a creep like that?" she exclaimed. "You've got to be
joking!" and once again Martin's heart warmed towards such
perspicacity in one so young. "No," she hastened to explain, "I
only met him the once, and why I chatted him up, it was so's
he could fill me in about the job. You know; what it was like,
kind of thing. What *you* were like. To work for, I mean." She
paused. "He said you were okay," she concluded, tolerantly,
"except when you were in one of your moods."

In one of my moods! Martin almost choked with fury.

"What Mr. Cummings is pleased to describe as 'one of my
moods,'" he explained coldly, "refer without exception to those
numerous occasions when he has let me down without warning
and for reasons so trivial as to be nothing short of downright
insolence. Now I hope, Ruth, that if we *do* decide to take you
on, you'll put your back into the work, make a decent job of it.
I can't afford to have *another* assistant mucking me about,
missing appointments, upsetting my schedules. I hope that's
understood? If you do a job for me, you'll do it well and thoroughly? Right?"

"Oh yes. I'll do it well and thoroughly, all right," she assured
him; and for a moment it seemed to Martin that she was mak-

ing the words sound like some kind of a threat: but of course
that was ridiculous. "So don't worry about that, Mr. Lockwood. There's just one more thing, though—"

He was waiting for this. For some minutes now Martin had
been turning over in his mind how to break it to her about the
80p an hour. Not that this was the way the Grants people put
the case to aspiring employees: £3.00 per interview was the
figure they quoted, with little congratulatory squeals for the
lucky applicant about to lay his hands on such loot. But 80p
an hour was what it actually came to, by the time you'd
telephoned your subject to fix an appointment, had found your
way to his address at No. 144 on some God-forsaken Council
Estate, with all the doorways labelled 1–11, and then waited
around until he came back from the doctor's, the dry-cleaners,
the betting-shop; and then, on top of all that, actually *getting*
the interview, typing it out when you got home, pages of it,
sometimes, half of it illegible and having to be filled in out of
your own head. . . .

How to present all this enticingly, that was the problem.
Martin decided on the detached, breezy approach. If all else
failed, he could top-up the meagre pittance from his own
pocket: it would be uneconomic, but worth it, in the way that
champagne is uneconomic but worth it, or a weekend in a five-
star hotel.

"About money," he began, "I have to warn you, Ruth, that
the rates we can afford to pay—that the Grants Committee
can afford to pay, that is, it's not really anything to do with
me—"

She interrupted him.

"Who said anything about paying? I don't want any pay. I'll
get you your interviews for nothing."

In a way, it was wonderful. In a way, it solved everything,
particularly the problem of how the Grants people would view
the prospect of allotting him a second assistant. "But you've
got Walter Cummings already," they'd say, looking it up in

their filing system under C. And if he suggested scrapping
Walter and replacing him by this obviously more efficient
young woman, their eyes would widen reproachfully. "But
don't you realise, Mr. Lockwood, that Walter comes from a
Broken Home!" they'd say, in hushed voices, as if he'd
switched on an electric razor in church: and if (as had once
happened) he allowed himself to retort that he wasn't surprised, Walter was enough to break any home, they'd gasp in
horror, as if he were Crippen himself, and he would practically
hear his prospects of promotion clanging yet another notch or
two downwards.

So Ruth Ledbetter's unprecedented quixotry was in one way
a godsend. In another, it was slightly unnerving.

If she wasn't in it for the money, then what *was* she in it
for?

"I'm just interested," she explained smugly. "Any objec-
tions?"

Lots: but Martin couldn't think how to put them into
words. What they added up to was a profound and all-embracing mistrust of people who act from motives other than those
of self-interest. Such people weren't playing fair, it always
seemed to Martin, and dealing with them was like playing
chess according to a revised set of rules known only to your op-
ponent: defeat is certain. Unselfish people are frightening, he
felt, in the same way that lunatics are frightening; you never
know what they may do next.

On the other hand, this Ruth Ledbetter didn't *look* like an
unselfish person. The narrowed eyes, watching him, were
shrewd and sharp; the small mouth had a greedy look about it,
which Martin found obscurely reassuring. You just couldn't
imagine this girl doing good for its own sake, though of course
good of a sort, for somebody—maybe for Martin Lockwood?—
might easily emerge as a by-product of her activities. Thus
might a famous surgeon cure people of their cancers, not in

order to cure them of their cancers but in order to become a famous surgeon.

But who cares? Certainly not the lucky patients.

"I think we are going to make a good team, Ruth," he said carefully, "I think we are going to understand one another. Now, come over here, and let me explain to you exactly what it is I am trying to do."

CHAPTER 13

"A bit short on plot, aren't you?" she commented, slapping Section III down on top of the pile. "When's something going to *happen?*" and then she listened attentively, just as if she hadn't known she was talking rubbish, while he explained that this wasn't a work of fiction, but a factual scientific study.

"You could have fooled me," she remarked, and then: "I thought fact was supposed to be stranger than fiction? How come *your* facts aren't? Where do you *find* such boring facts, anyway? D'you advertise, or something?—'Boring Facts Wanted for Academic Do-Or-Die Sale. Outworn Ideas and Second-Hand Theories of All Kinds, for Sale or Exchange. Jargon, Platitudes, and Miscellaneous Gobbledygook for Fancy-That Stall . . .'"

"Look, Ruth, it's all very well to laugh. You don't seem to understand at all the way a research project like this has to be mounted. You see—"

"Sorry, Prof! I'm kinda fooling. Like, you drive me to it some way, did you know that? Thing is, I'm an academic really, just like you, and I can't stand to see a good subject go to waste. Depression *is* a good subject. A *bloody* good subject. Real sick. But the way you handle it, it's like the Bluebeard story if she hadn't got around to unlocking the forbidden door. Just, he came home and said 'There's a good girl, I knew I could rely on you,' and they'd sat down to supper and lived happily ever after.

"You see, Prof, I *know* about depression. Like, I was the one who unlocked the door and was there waiting when Bluebeard got home. I tell you, Prof—Oh, *shit!*"

The sound of the telephone startled Martin, too, but Ruth was on her feet first, and rushing across the room. She snatched up the receiver, and a few seconds later laid it down, gently.

"A wrong number," she reported off-handedly, coming back to her seat; and Martin didn't argue. In a way, he wished everyone would handle telephone calls this way. It would add years to one's life.

"Bluebeard?" he prompted her, as she settled back in the big chair, legs tucked beneath her. "You were talking about Bluebeard." He didn't want her to lose the thread just when it was beginning to get interesting. His mid-morning boredom had shrunk to a tiny dot, on the very edge of consciousness, and he wanted it to stay that way. "About opening the door into the closet," he continued, "or the attic, or whatever the hell it was . . . ?"

Irritatingly, Ruth shook her head.

"You should have listened to me last night," she reminded him smugly; and though Martin felt damn sure that she hadn't said anything about Bluebeard last night—it would have roused him, surely, if she'd used a bit of vocabulary that much off the beaten track?—he let it pass.

Besides, she was obviously dying to tell him. A moment later she was talking again.

"You poor sods with your degrees," she said. "You've blinded yourselves with print so's you can't see *people* any more at all. Instead of facts, you just see long words sprouting above their collars. You talk to me about facts, but actually you aren't seeing any facts at all, just print and typing paper and carbon. I'll tell you something, Prof. The facts about depression *are* stranger than fiction. One hell of a lot stranger. If you looked, like I've looked, then you'd see what I see. And *then* you'd have a thesis to write, by God you would! Bluebeard wouldn't be in it, nor Dracula either. Well, yes, perhaps

Dracula. We'll make an exception of Dracula, right? You'd see why if you'd listened to what I told you last night. About my mother. Remember what I said about my mother?"

Her mother . . . her mother. She *had* said something . . . but then they all said things about their mothers, the same things, over and over, how could he be expected to distinguish one mother from another? Too protective . . . too indifferent. Too strict . . . too permissive. Too loving . . . too unloving. Too sluttish . . . too houseproud. By now, Martin had an actual picture in his mind of this composite creature, this amalgam of incompatible qualities: a large, amorphous oblong, slow-moving and vaguely transparent, somewhat like a jelly-fish in texture, you could prod it into any shape you liked with the ball of your thumb.

"Your mother. Ah, yes," he said. "She took away your confidence, wasn't that it?" Surely he was on pretty safe ground here?

"No, she did not!" Ruth retorted sharply. "You've got it all wrong. *I* took away *her* confidence. And you know how I did it? I used to give her depressions. Like you might give someone an injection of paraldehyde. Right?"

Right. That it could hardly be. Wrong, surely, by any ordinary standards? Or maybe she was just pulling his leg? But right, no.

Still, he didn't want to slap her down as she deserved, not yet, anyway. The bizarre interchange was really doing him good, he hadn't felt as well as this in months. Maybe the human intellect *needs* a certain amount of nonsense, like roughage, to render the slabs of hard, established fact digestible?

Hoping for further mild shock-therapy, Martin played her along, as in a depth-interview.

"Your mother," he repeated. "You used to give her depressions." He kept his voice carefully non-judgemental, in the approved manner. "Now, why did you do that?"

"*Why?* To punish her, of course," said Ruth. "I'd have thought that was obvious."

"Ah. Yes. To punish her." Martin paused, radiating non-surprise at the top of his bent. "Punish her for what?" He made the question sound casual, an afterthought.

"For *what?* For being my mother, of course!" Ruth snapped. "What more do you need?" and while Martin was thinking out a suitably non-judgemental answer to this one, Ruth forestalled him with a further question:

"Aren't you going to ask me how I did it?" she demanded, in a slightly aggrieved voice, as if he had omitted some essential courtesy, like saying "Please," or "Thank you." "Go on, ask me how I did it!" and without waiting for him to comply, she continued:

"The first time I did it, it was kind of an accident, like that bloke in history, or is it literature, who invented roast pork by burning a house down with a pig inside. That's how it was for me the first time, but after a bit I found it didn't have to be such a big deal. I found I'd kinda learned the knack; you do, you know, like with killing a chicken, you don't need to use much force at all, just the right kind of flick of the wrist. I could put her in a depression just whenever I liked. She couldn't make it out at first, what was happening, because I was being ever such a good daughter to her at that point; but after a while the penny dropped, and she got real scared of having me around. It got so she wouldn't let me into the house; changed the locks, all that jazz, but it didn't matter because by that time I'd found I could do it from a distance just as easily. Tele-damage, you might say. Like I'd got her wavelength kind of thing, I could tap her from anywhere. . . .

"It's a sort of faith-healing in reverse, you see. The laying-on of hands. At first, you actually do have to lay your hands on the person, that's why she thought what a loving daughter I'd turned into, hugging and stroking her; but after a bit they get kind of sensitised to you, and you can do it to them even down the telephone.

"Look, Prof, do me a favour. Take that look off your face. Faith-healing's *respectable* these days, hadn't you noticed? It's in the learned journals as well as on telly, the Russians are into it too, it's a military thing over there, and so it's got to be serious, right? Even the medicos are falling over themselves to believe in it. They have faith-healers on the wards of the big teaching hospitals like mascots, to prove how up-to-the-minute they are. Remember that comparative study reported in the British Medical News where they measured the rate of healing of fractures when . . ."

"Of course I remember," snapped Martin, meaning not that he remembered (how should he?) but that he could well believe it, you could get away with anything these days provided only that you could somehow get in with the editors of the relevant journal. "But I don't see," he objected, "how this has got anything to do with my survey? It's *depression* I'm working on. Not fractures."

" 'Not fractures.' " She mimicked his dismissive tone. "Nor hernias either. Nor detached retinas. Okay? It's the *principle* of the thing I'm trying to explain to you, Prof. Like I was trying to explain it to you last night."

She giggled. "It was 'sleep-deprivation' prevented you listening to me that time. And so what is it that's preventing you now? Like, isn't there *any* time in the twenty-four hours when you're capable of giving your mind to *anything?*"

Wasn't there? The question didn't bear thinking about.

"Go on," he said, grudgingly: and on, almost too fluently, she went.

And on, and on. She was loving it; and so, to his growing amazement was he. Lunch was forgotten, and though it was nearly four o'clock before she finally left, he found himself actually sorry to see her go.

This was a new experience to him. He couldn't remember, ever before, having felt other than pleased—nay, delighted—to see a visitor go, even after an hour or so; and this had been five hours, at least.

Something cataclysmic had happened to him, the implications of which he was only now beginning, dimly, to comprehend.

And so it came about that when Helen arrived home an hour or so later, she found her lover not merely not in a coma or dead, as the staffroom speculations might have led one to suppose, but pounding away at the typewriter in such a trance of inspiration as she had never before witnessed, and had scarcely dared to hope for. She had heard the muted thunder of it while still coming up the stairs, but had not believed her ears. Entering the flat, and finding her wildest hopes confirmed, her first thought was to avoid interrupting him, and she had tiptoed reverently past the open sitting-room door, almost choked with relief and with joy that somehow, from somewhere, he had found the inspiration so long and so desperately sought.

What could she cook that might worthily celebrate this miraculous turn of events? All her weariness gone, her feet no longer aching as they skimmed back and forth across the kitchen lino, Helen's mind was in a turmoil of love, and pride, and special white-wine sauces, and she knew, as one sometimes does, that this was an evening she would remember for the rest of her days.

CHAPTER 14

The first inkling Helen had that something other than sponta-
neous inspiration was at the back of Martin's extraordinary
transformation was when Beatrice phoned, early the next
morning. Like most Other Women and the corresponding
wives, Helen and Beatrice had started off with the tacit determination to cut one another dead on all occasions. This always
looks, on the face of it, to be far the most dignified course, as
well as the least painful all round: but in the event it nearly always turns out to be sadly impractical. Sooner or later the war-
ring pair are forced into communication, if only to determine
the whereabouts of the loved one's thick pullover, or to attempt to shuffle off responsibility for housing his six-foot-high
steel filing-cabinet among the knickknacks in the sitting-room.
Mostly, this sort of thing can be debated over the telephone,
icily, and with due regard to the current state of hostilities; but
sooner or later the time comes when a face-to-face confron-
tation becomes unavoidable, and the two are compelled to
meet. This first meeting is usually embarked on with the
avowed intention of quarrelling; but all too easily this initial
determination slides over almost imperceptibly into mutual
condolences about the by-now evident shortcomings of their
shared mate, and an uneasy kind of rapport can spring up
which it is impossible to categorise. You can't call it friendship
when the participants are so evidently enemies, and when the
only reason they have made contact at all is on account of the
harm they are doing each other, and will continue to do.

Nevertheless, something *has* grown between them, in the

teeth of all expectation—and indeed all intention—to the contrary, and a point comes when both begin to realise, albeit below the level of consciousness, that they would be lost without each other. Their long-standing mutual hostility begins to seem like the one firm rock amid the turmoil of change that is breaking over both their heads. "At least she still hates me," they can reassure themselves, "so I must be doing *something* right."

Thus it was not altogether surprising that Beatrice, in her indignation and bewilderment that morning, should turn to Helen to confide in—to have a row with—something. Of course, for decency's sake, she pretended that she was startled and taken-aback that it should be Helen and not Martin who picked up the phone: but what else, actually, could she have expected at this hour? She'd been married to Martin, after all, for fourteen years, 365 mornings per year, plus three extra for leap-years.

"That bloody girl!" she spluttered; and, "Speaking," said Helen resignedly before she'd had time to think about it, and to realise that the remark, being in the third person, could not properly be referring to herself. "Sorry—I mean this is Helen. Did you want to speak to Martin? He's still asleep, I'm afraid. He had rather a late night last night . . ."

It was true. The strange, demonic energy which had had him in its grip when Helen had arrived home, had lasted all evening, and far into the night. For hours he'd crouched over the typewriter, tense and purposeful as an athlete on the starting-line, bashing at the keys with two fingers like one possessed, pausing only occasionally to dash off a few notes, huge dramatic scrawls from a thick felt pen, slanting across the page like streaks of black lightning. Then back to the typing again, the noise of the keys racing against some invisible clock inside his head, until Helen herself began to feel breathless, as if she had been running up hill all evening long. At one point, she'd thought he wasn't even going to stop for the specially prepared dinner, and was torn between disappointment that she'd gone to all that trouble for nothing, and joy that his inspiration should have so completely taken over. In the end, he had knocked off for long enough to eat the meal, though he brought his papers to table and scarcely spoke to her while he ate.

Helen was not affronted by this: it was wonderful. She could tell, too, by the way he forked it into his mouth, that he was, on some level, enjoying the food. In its small way, it was contributing to the ecstasies of creation, and Helen was proud and happy that this should be so.

Midnight. One o'clock. Two o'clock. In the end she had gone to bed without him, and had fallen asleep to the ongoing sound of the typewriter pounding triumphantly through the small-hours.

"Can I give him a message?" she said to Beatrice, settling the receiver in her left hand and reaching for pencil and paper with her right. "I'd rather not wake him if you don't mind, because you see . . ."

"A message! Yes, you bloody *can* give him a message!" and Helen sat, pencil poised. "You can tell him, from me, that if he wants to make beastly disgusting unfair insinuations against me, he can bloody well make them himself, to my face, and not send that sneaky, two-faced lying little bitch to do his dirty work for him! I've had enough of her, tell him! That's the *second* time! If she comes to the house again, tell him, she'll get a jug of cold water in her face! I mean it! I've got it standing just inside the door, all ready . . . !"

Helen's brain was spinning. "Look, Beatrice, I'm sorry; I'm sorry you're upset, but I don't know *what* you're talking about. *What* girl . . . ?"

"How do *I* know what girl? I don't know anything about his girls any more, why should I, that's *your* worry now, thank goodness, not mine! But when it comes to sending them round here, casting horrible aspersions, absolutely unjustified, not a

word of truth in them . . . ! 'A Parasite Person,' that's what
she called me, if you please! A *Parasite! Me.* And it's not even
as if I was *getting* the bloody alimony yet, it may be months,
my solicitor says! A Parasite, indeed! How would *you* like it, a
sly, foul-mouthed little bitch hardly out of her teens standing
there in your own drawing-room calling you names like that?"

"Well, I wouldn't," said Helen reasonably. "I'd be very annoyed. I'd ask them what they meant by it—what it was all
about? Look, Beatrice, she must have said *something* . . .
Didn't you even find out her name . . . ?"

"Oh, her *name!* And what's the use of *that*, I'd like to know,
when I'd never heard of her in my life before? Ruth, she called
herself. Ruth-bloody-Leadswinger or something of the sort, in
case that leaves you any the wiser, it doesn't me . . . !"

In Helen's mind, everything suddenly clicked into place.
The Ledbetter interview. Ruth Ledbetter, the girl Martin had
interviewed in hospital after her suicide attempt. So *that's* who
it was who'd turned up so mysteriously in the middle of the
night, and had seemed so mysteriously familiar. It was her style
of speech that was familiar, not her person: all those slangy ab-
breviations and throwaway Americanisms that had been so
wearisome to decipher and transcribe.

So she'd visited Beatrice, too, uninvited? What was she up
to? What was going on?

"Look, Beatrice," she was beginning; but suddenly the
phone went dead. She had been cut off—or was it merely a
fault on the line?

Hastily dialling the once-forbidden number—it still felt peculiar, and rather wicked, like steaming-open a letter—Helen
rang back; but it was no use, she just got the engaged signal.

Perhaps Beatrice was ringing *her* back? Better give it a
chance.

Perhaps Beatrice, too, was giving it a chance? They could go
on like this for ever. Helen shrugged, noted that it was by now
well past eight, and hurried into the kitchen. If Martin wasn't
going to wake up before she left—and it looked as if he wasn't

—then there was still a chance of getting to school nice and early, like yesterday. Also like yesterday—it now occurred to her—she'd have yet another amusing anecdote to tell.

The ex-wife's irate phone-call. The identity of the mysterious midnight visitor. They'd love it.

Indeed they did love it: and of course none of them—least of all Helen—had any idea of just how much these snippets of light entertainment were going to cost, and to whom.

CHAPTER 15

"The rôle of the Parasite Person in the Aetiology of Endogenous Depression" was his provisional title. It had come to him during yesterday's unprecedented bout of galloping creation, and this morning, to his intense relief, it still looked good.

This was not always the case, as he well remembered. Even in the old days, when his creative powers had seemed to be at their zenith, even then an idea that had seemed to be of world-shaking brilliance and originality in the small-hours would sometimes dwindle, under the harsh morning light, into a mere jumble of pretentious platitudes, leading nowhere. Remembering this, he had woken this morning in a sweat of terror lest just this should have happened now; that all those pages of typescript reeled off in the white-heat of inspiration, all evening and half the night, should prove to be just one more sleep-crazed delusion, destined, by daylight, for the dustbin. So great had been this fear that he had lain for more than an hour, eyes closed, imagining himself still asleep, imagining himself still dreaming, imagining himself suddenly dead of a heart-attack—*anything* to put off the moment of intolerable disillusionment which lurked—Did it? Didn't it?—among that uncorrected, unexamined mound of typescript on his desk.

He had heard the alarm clock go all right; had felt the soft creaking of Helen getting out of bed, trying not to wake him; had been aware of her soft, considerate drifts of movement around the flat as she got herself ready for work; and finally—

what he'd been waiting for all along—he heard at last the careful closing of the front door that meant she had really gone.

And only now, alone with his destiny, did he feel he had it in him to leave his bed and set off on the awful voyage of discovery into the sitting-room.

It was all right! It was *all right!* The briefest glance through last night's outpourings showed him that his creative excitement had not, after all, been illusory. He was on to something, he really was; something new, and exciting, and wildly controversial, exactly as he'd always dreamed. And the title was perfect, couched as it was in acceptably scholarly form, and yet provoking curiosity far beyond the drily academic. The common reader—even the commonest of them—would surely find himself at least momentarily intrigued and titillated?

Parasite Persons. The phrase had been Ruth's in the first place, though it was not she who had thought it would make a good title. It didn't, she pointed out thoughtfully, kinda grab you. Not unless you knew what parasites *were*.

"Like, give the poor devil a break who designs the book-jacket," she urged. "And the publicity stuff too, for the movie, you don't want to forget that. It's kinda not very photogenic, is it, a parasite? Not when you come to really think about it; how many legs it has, that sort of thing. Like, is it bug-eyed, tentacles, all that stuff? Or bi-focals and a stuffed shirt? See what I mean?"

Martin saw. And what he saw thrilled him to the very marrow. Book-jackets! Film adaptations! This girl was thinking for him thoughts which he himself hadn't dared to think in years! She moved among his most secret ambitions as if this was her native habitat, thus giving them a sort of substance, a legitimate place in the map of the future. It was wonderful. It was like nothing he had ever experienced before, and he found himself riveted by her every word.

"How about *Vampires Anonymous?*" she suggested, as they sat drinking to the new venture in vodka, having missed their lunch. "Anyone can draw a vampire. You know. Fangs, and blood dripping from them, that kind of thing."

Was it the case that "anyone" could draw a vampire? Martin felt very sure that he himself couldn't, he'd have no idea at all how to start. Did the thing have wings, and if so were they vaguely like a bat's? And how did they fold up, straight down the sides, obscuring the arms, or crossed-over at the back, like a swift or a house-martin?

Still, no point in accentuating the age-gap by admitting to such ignorance, so he gave a grunt of non-committal encouragement.

"*Vampires Anonymous* by Martin Lockwood," Ruth declaimed gleefully, downing the remains of her vodka. "How does *that* sound?"

It sounded just fine: but not in the least like a PhD thesis by a respected lecturer in Social Psychology. There was no way Dr. Frost was going to accept such a title, no matter how unexceptionable might be the material subsumed thereunder.

And, of course, the material *wasn't* going to be unexceptionable. That was the whole point of the thing. It wasn't until Ruth had taken herself off, a little before four, that Martin, alone at last with his thoughts, began fully to realise the immensity of the thing that had happened; that within his grasp, at long last, was the new and revolutionary hypothesis for which he had so desperately been seeking. Vampires or Parasites—who cared? It was the *idea* that was going to count; the startling—and surely original?—idea that depression is not an illness at all, but a crime. A crime perpetrated by one person upon another from motives of personal gain. Like burglary. In fact, it *was* burglary, on the psycho-somatic level. It was theft, the appropriation by one person of another's energy and joy in living, which the thief then stores away for his own use, leaving the victim an empty husk, a hollow ghost of a person, without joy, without zest, and incapable any longer of carrying on successfully either his work or his social life.

"Show me a depressive," Ruth had said, at some stage during the long, extraordinary afternoon, "and I'll show you a Parasite Person. A buoyant, cheerful, outgoing type, with sympathy and kindness coming out of their ears, and devoting an amazing amount of time and trouble to 'cheering up' the poor bloody victim.

"Wonderful, wonderful people, everyone's going to say, so kind, so patient, falling over backwards to try and help the ungrateful depressive, pulling out all the stops—care, compassion, the lot. And all the while they are growing fat on the happiness and hope they are quietly draining out of their victim. You see them growing popular, successful; admired by tapping their victim's zest and energy and enthusiasm, and diverting it into themselves. Like you could pipe-off someone's water-supply from higher up the stream, and if it didn't occur to them to go and look, they'd just think the stream had run dry.

"That's what they *do* think, most of them," Ruth had continued. "They think they've run dry because their mothers didn't breast-feed them, or because Vietnam was all their fault, or because they aren't drinking skim-milk, or decaffeinated grape-juice, or some damnfool thing or other. And when that doesn't work, they go running to a doctor, who'll send them to a shrink, and he'll give them some bottles of pills and a whole load of new things to think it's because of.

"And all the time, of course, they shouldn't be going to the medical profession at all, they should be going to the police. Dialling 999. That sort of thing. That's what you do when you find you've been robbed. . . ."

It was fascinating. Martin tried to visualise the reactions of a policeman to such a summons; or the girl on the end of 999 come to that. He had his notebook out by now, writing down the best bits, and wondering, with a peculiar, mounting excitement, what in the world he was going to do with them.

Because it was all nonsense, obviously. The scientist in him was growing more and more queasy with every paragraph; and yet for some reason he was unable to think of any precise grounds for rejecting the whole thing out of hand. There was nothing you could pin down quantitatively of course, to prove or disprove such a theory, but that was often the case, it didn't get you anywhere. Really, it was the general implausibility of the thing that condemned it, together with the impossibility of testing it. What sort of an experiment could you set up? Where would you find your controls? How define your Parasite Person to exclude ordinary, bona fide helpers and sympathisers?

"There *are* no bona fide helpers and sympathisers," Ruth countered dogmatically. "Anyone who voluntarily stays around a depressive is doing it for what he can get. Though of course he has to give something too, up to a point, just like a farmer has to feed his cows if he wants to get the milk and the lovely lovely meat, right?

"It's a con trick, you see, ladling out sympathy and patience like ladling pig-swill into the trough. Along comes the pig, squealing with joy and gratitude, but only because he's never heard of bacon. . . ."

Some good quotes here, undoubtedly. Martin was getting it all down verbatim now, and thoroughly enjoying himself.

But all the same, it would not do. No way.

"The trouble is," he said, "that intriguing though all this may be in theory, you haven't got one scrap of evidence that anything of the sort actually happens. Nor do I see how you can get any. All right, so you might be able to show that many depressives—most of them, if you like *do* tend to have some character around who goes in for acting supportive, cheering them up, and so forth. Even going to extraordinary lengths to do so, like that Timberley couple—you've read that one, have you?" He gestured towards the pile of completed interviews through which, at his instigation, Ruth had been leafing.

She looked up, suddenly alert, her whole body tense and eager, like a hound that has just picked up the scent.

"The Timberleys! Now there you are! An archetypal example of just exactly what I've been saying! Here we have the

greedy, hungry, compassionate old man living off his immobilised old wife like a tapeworm off its host! How cheerful
he was, according to your record, how optimistic, in the face of
his frightful situation! What a wonderful husband, the neighbours were no doubt saying. But didn't it strike you to wonder
how he could keep it up? Where it all came from, the stamina
to actually *enjoy* his hideous life? It came from *her*, of course.
Read through this stuff again, and you'll see that it's *her* energy, *her* cheerfulness that he's living on, fastening himself on
to her like a maggot on a piece of rotten meat. And everyone
looking on, meantime, and saying how saintly he is!

"Now, *that* would be a test case, Prof, if it's tests you're
wanting. Listen: how about if I was to get Mr. T. the Tapeworm out of that house for half a week, and how about if Mrs.
T. was to be on her feet by the end of that time, chatting with
the neighbours, cleaning the place up, off to Bingo, that sort of
thing? Would *that* count as evidence? Would it? Would it?"

Against his better judgement, Martin was impressed.

"If that *were* to happen, one would indeed begin to—But
look, Ruth; it won't do, it really won't. Just *one* case can't be
cited as evidence of anything, no matter how remarkable it
may be in itself. One would need a series of such cases, the
whole thing carefully set-up, with proper controls. Otherwise—
well, okay, you might get the odd case-history startling enough
to impress the layman, but unless the numbers were large
enough to be statistically significant. . . ."

"How much?" she asked sharply, like a skinflint housewife at
a market stall. "Out of these sixty-four subjects that we have to
interview, how many would have to recover dramatically after
the removal of their Parasite Person, before it would be
counted as 'statistically significant'?"

Martin hesitated. Statistics were tricky things, and a lot
depended on the particular editor, and on the power currently
wielded by those likely to be ranged against whatever it was
you were trying to prove.

"Six?" Ruth suggested tensely. "Eight?"

Still Martin would not commit himself. Certainly, six or eight case-histories of instant cures such as Ruth was envisaging would make *some* impact: If not in academic circles, then certainly in the popular press, if you could once get the facts through to them. It was the kind of hypothesis that would catch on. There is a paranoiac streak in almost everyone, not least in depressives, and the notion that their troubles were all someone's fault, and that they were being literally battened-on by their nearest and dearest, could become the big craze of the decade.

The rationale of it, though. *Some* sort of explanation would have to be adumbrated as to how the transaction could possibly take place. One person's energy being physically misappropriated by another—it all sounded too airy-fairy for words, even by today's permissive standards of scholarship. "Tapping" energies; "Draining away" happiness; as if it was gas or electricity, and plugging it into your own mains . . . This was science fiction stuff. Too intrinsically improbable to warrant serious investigation.

It's not *fair*, was his next thought, like a child deprived of an ice cream. In the field of astronomy they were allowed—nay, encouraged—to investigate things far more intrinsically improbable than anything Ruth had dreamed-up. Solar Wind, Galactic Noise, the Black Holes, the Expanding Universe, the Red Dwarfs, the White Dwarfs, the Supernovae—and no one ever demanded of *them* an explanation of why the uinverse should be like this rather than like something else. It just *is*, would be the smug reply, and what lucky, lucky people you are to have us here to tell you so.

And the sub-atomic physicists, even more so. They only had to come upon a particle that contravened the known laws of physics, and, as if butter wouldn't melt in their mouths, they altered the known laws of physics accordingly.

Why couldn't the Social Sciences be more like that? It was most inequitable; but there you were. You had to take your chosen discipline as you found it and play the game according to the rules. Unless, of course, you became one of the giants, like Freud, and invented a new game which caught on because it was more fun to play, and thereafter, as the inventor, you were allowed to make up the rules as you went along. Martin's mouth fairly watered at the mere thought of it.

Aloud, he summarised to Ruth such of these meditations as seemed relevant to her project.

"And so you see," he finished, "even if we ended up with quite a number of case-histories illustrating your point, it still wouldn't get us anywhere, unless we could come up with some plausible explanation as to how it actually, physically happens. Without that, they'll naturally . . ."

"I told you. Faith-healing," interrupted Ruth impatiently. "Faith-healing turned predator. I don't understand why you're so surprised; it's merely a criminal instead of a benevolent use of an established mechanism. It's always happening. Like a cash-register is designed for giving people the exact right change, but once you understand it, it can be used just as easily for cheating them. I know. I've done it. Why should you think it's so impossible for the same sort of thing to happen in the psychological field? What's so unlikely about it? People are like that."

Martin's mind was in a whirl. He no longer knew what he believed. For a moment, he felt that he was undergoing the Temptation in the Wilderness; but then suddenly it was a wilderness no longer, but a rich and virgin land, burgeoning with ideas of unprecedented brilliance and with new-minted facts sprouting up like dragons' teeth, everywhere, in a buzzing, blooming confusion.

CHAPTER 16

"She lives upon his shrieks and cries,
And she grows young as he grows
old."

It was amazing, now that he knew exactly what he was trying
to prove, how everything seemed to fall into place around it, as
if by magic. Relevant and supportive material simply flowed
into his mind, effortlessly, from every imaginable direction, all
of it ready-shaped, in some extraordinary way, for inclusion in
this whole, vast, exciting structure that was taking shape inside
his head.

This quotation from Blake, for instance. He hadn't read
Blake in years, not since O-levels, and he could have sworn
that every line of the beastly stuff had been wiped from his
brain completely, like recovering from a fever, the moment the
exam was over.

But somehow, below the level of consciousness, and for
reasons unimaginable at the time, these two lines had been
stored away in his memory-bank all ready to emerge on cue at
this supreme moment, twenty-five years on, when his genius
was suddenly bursting into flower. If he was to use them in a
chapter heading—and how superbly appropriate they were!—
he must find out which poem they came from, give a proper
reference. Or get Helen to. She actually liked this sort of thing,
very likely knew the poem by heart already. Unless it was one
of those ghastly Visions, of course, hundreds of pages long, and
not much more comprehensible than a Punk Rock lyric.

Of course, Blake had been a manic-depressive. Interesting, that. Maybe he could use it some way? It would be a matter of locating the Parasite Person in Blake's life, and establishing some sort of correlation between the bouts of depression and the presence of this person in his vicinity.

The wife was the most likely candidate. Mrs. Blake must have been one of those tolerant, supportive people because of that anecdote of the two of them playing Adam and Eve stark naked in a summerhouse—he remembered the whole Fifth Form guffawing over it—and for a woman of those days to co-operate in such an adventure, what with servants and neighbours and everything, she'd need to be very supportive indeed. Just the type to qualify as a Parasite Person. *Did* Blake's depressions seem to be worse when she was around; better when she wasn't, when she was away visiting, or having a baby, or whatever? If only some sort of statistical correlation could be established, from letters and diaries and stuff . . . The idea excited him considerably, until it occurred to him what an awful lot of reading would be involved—all those great, fat biographies, it was just too daunting. Of course, Helen could do the reading for him, she often did, when he couldn't be bothered with some ghastly great tome; and he had to hand it to her, she was an adept at extracting the sense from such a volume and handing it to him on two neatly-typed quarto pages. But in order to exercise this invaluable talent she needed, naturally, to know exactly what Martin was getting at, and for some reason which he preferred not to analyse he didn't want Helen to know anything at all about what was going on in his mind just now. That *something* had suddenly inspired him during the past two or three days, she could not fail to be aware, what with his long, passionate sessions at the typewriter, his tranced, preoccupied air at mealtimes, his reluctance to leave his work and come to bed until far into the night.

She *must* have noticed the transformation; she must, in fact, be dying of curiosity about it; but, like the good girl she was,

she asked no questions. Any other woman, he thought grate-
fully, would at least have done some heavy probing by now:
"How's it going, darling?" "Is it working out at last?"—that
kind of thing.

She was a wonderful girl, really; wonderful at helping, and
wonderful, too, at leaving you alone. A rare combination.

So, what with one thing and another, he decided to shelve
Blake for the moment. Apart from anything else, there was no
knowing where such a project would end. Because if Blake,
then why not Tolstoy? Or Meredith? Or Tennyson? Depressed
geniuses were two-a-penny during the nineteenth century, and
most of them had self-sacrificing, supportive wives, who could
well be Parasite Persons. They lived so bloody *long*, too, and
even the ones who mercifully didn't, like Keats, or Schubert,
didn't really give you any kind of a break, because all that happened was that the biographer would set himself to make a
meal of the few years available, so that there would still be
nine hundred pages or so to slog through.

So that line of research was out, at least until Helen had
been brought in on the project. But no matter. Other ideas,
even better, and more brilliant, were already surging through
his mind, faster than he could get them down.

It was like being young again. He had forgotten it could feel
like this, his brain so light, so swift, fitting his skull so exactly,
no weight, no pressures anywhere, no blanks, no gaps, no areas
of darkness or muddle. His mind was darting hither and
thither, like a lizard in the noonday sun, snatching at everything, rejecting nothing, relying absolutely on some mighty
synthesising power within him to make sense of it all, to notice
correspondences among all this disparate material where none
had ever been noticed before.

"Faith-Healing and Human Evolution" he wrote, and in his
excitement underlined it three times, in the blackest of black
ink. Because Ruth was quite right: faith-healing *had* become
respectable over the last few years. He'd spent all yesterday af-

ternoon in the Medical Reference Library, and had succeeded in running to earth no less than a dozen articles on the subject in perfectly respectable learned journals; and though not all of them came down on the side of the magicians, they were all serious studies by serious and reputable authors with strings of okay letters after their names. Alternative Medicine, it seemed, was fast coming in out of the cold, with Martin Lockwood hot on its heels and about to overtake it.

The introduction of Natural Selection into the argument was going to be his *pièce de résistance*. As Ruth had so rightly insisted, if faith-healing works at all, then it must work in both directions. Whatever is the mechanism by which you can pour health and vigour into another person, by that same mechanism you must be able to draw it out, and the exciting thing was that if you believed in Natural Selection at all, then the latter capacity must by now be far more highly evolved than the former.

"Look at it this way," Martin found himself scribbling, in this first, headlong draft, "if there *is* in the human animal this capacity to transfer health and energy from one individual to another, then it is perfectly clear that the selective advantage of this capacity will lie not with those individuals who use it to benefit others at their own expense (the Faith-healers), but rather with those who use it for the reverse purpose, namely, to draw out the energy from their neighbours and use it for themselves. With the passing of the millennia, would you not expect these latter individuals—those who used their power selfishly—to have left more progeny than those who used it unselfishly? Thus it seems reasonable to believe that, whatever number of successful faith-healers may now exist among us, they must by now be far outnumbered by their opposite numbers, the Parasite Persons . . ."

The elaboration of this idea filled several pages, and by the end of them Martin had the whole of Evolution ranged solidly on his side: no small achievement. He had proved to his own satisfaction that, by the processes of natural selection, this kind of psycho-somatic parasitism must have spread through human population like, geologically speaking, wildfire; and must still be spreading. And as the numbers of the Parasite Persons increase, so, *pari passu* must the numbers of their victims, i.e. the Depressives. And, lo and behold, is it not the case that depression *is* on the increase nowadays . . . ?

And so there! Q.E.D.! Hooray, hooray, hooray!

Martin drew a line, with a great flourish, under this section, and felt like dancing round and round the room.

But not yet . . . not yet. More ideas were coming . . . more and more of them . . . each one seemed to be burning a hole in his brain like money in the pocket of a spendthrift. He must get them down on paper, fast . . . fast . . . !

All those depressed geniuses, whose Lives he couldn't for the moment be bothered with, Tolstoy and so on? They were depressed, weren't they, because of the depredations of the Parasite Persons around them. Yes, okay, but *why* did they so consistently have such persons attached to them? Answer: Because a Parasite Person, like any other thief, chooses a rich victim rather than a poor one to rob. It's common sense. And since great men are, by their very nature, exceptionally rich in all the qualities—energy, zest and so on—which the parasites are most eager to steal, these are the victims they prefer to set upon, just as a professional burglar prefers to set his sights on a film-star loaded with diamonds. . . .

The whole thing hung together incredibly well, especially when you took into account the fact that these Parasites, like any other criminal, vary widely in their degree of skill and daring. Some—and these correspond to sneak-thieves and pickpockets—are capable of snatching only a little, and only rarely, from their undistinguished victims; and in these cases, the effects are barely noticeable. At the other end of the scale, however, are what you might call the big-time parasites, the really outstanding psycho-somatic criminals. . . .

Outstanding . . . Outstanding . . . Wasn't there a quotation from Adler illustrating what he was trying to say? Martin went to the bookshelf. Yes, that would be it: *The Science of Living*. Oddly, he could remember exactly where on the page the quote came, but had not the least idea of the context, or in which chapter it might be found. He persevered, however, flipping the pages back and forth, and was finally rewarded: here it was, the very paragraph he needed:

"If one person out of a family is more outstanding than the others, the latter will suffer. This is always so, whether the favoured individual be the father, one of the children, or the mother. A very difficult situation is created for the other members of the family, and sometimes they cannot bear it . . ."

Of course they cannot. They have among them a Parasite Person of such monstrous appetite that he or she is able to eat not just one of them alive, but all of them. A sort of caterpillar in the family, eating six times its own weight in food every day. A caterpillar nearly two yards high, up-ended, fully-dressed, prowling the stairs, the kitchen, the living-room . . .

Adler wasn't the only one. Once he got around to studying them, there'd be loads of authorities whose findings could be so interpreted as to support his thesis, in one way or another. There'd be Laing, for instance. Because sometimes the exact opposite of Adler's scenario can be observed, and a whole household of successful parasites will be found battening on a single depressive . . .

Altogether, Martin had a wonderful morning. Like police clearing the route for a royal procession, his mind was clearing away, briskly and efficiently, all the obstacles to the theory which had earlier seemed so insuperable. What was it he'd said to Ruth, only a couple of days ago? "It's a theory impossible to test," he'd complained to her. "What sort of experiment could you set up that could either confirm or refute it?"

How doltish he must have been, only that short time ago! Today, he could think straight off of half a dozen ingenious experiments, any one of which, properly monitored, might give positive results. You could, for instance, on some plausible pretext, do a few performance tests on the parasite figure—Memory, Creativity, I.Q. and so on. The results might reveal that his performance tended to be at its peak at just those times when his victim—the depressive, that is—was at his lowest ebb. A negative correlation here would be exciting indeed! A certain amount of preliminary data on these lines could be obtained by simple questioning of the parties concerned.

The questions must, on the face of it, seem perfectly innocent, of course: "At what time of day would you say you feel at your most energetic, most able to tackle difficult tasks?"—that sort of thing. And if the parasite figure, all unsuspecting, should more often than not reply "First thing in the morning," then you really *would* be on to something! For is it not an established fact, proven beyond all doubt, that this is the very time of day when depressions are almost universally at their worst?

If the results of this preliminary enquiry were to prove positive—and already it was beginning to seem inconceivable to Martin that they should not—then all sorts of supplementary investigations could be set in train to supply confirmatory data. His brain throbbed with the excitement of it, the certainty of success.

Anti-depressants: that could be one angle. Why are these drugs so notoriously unreliable, working splendidly for one patient, and yet failing dismally for another, with apparently identical symptoms? Or even in the case of the same patient, it can commonly happen that during one depressive episode he will do marvellously on these drugs, and then a few months later, presenting with identical symptoms and being prescribed the very same drug, he may this time experience no benefit whatsoever. Many are the doctors who have been baffled by these discrepancies, many the theories that have been vainly propounded; and now here was Martin Lockwood coming up with a new and arresting hypothesis that would explain it all!

The Parasite Person, of course! As fast as the anti-depressant begins to generate new energy in the patient, so fast likewise does the attendant parasite, the psychic tapeworm, devour it, sucking it out as fast as it is generated, leaving the victim as limp and listless as before. A study must immediately be mounted showing that these drugs only work reliably when the patient is free of his Parasite Person; when the latter is sick, or away on holiday, or for some other reason temporarily absent. It should not be difficult to establish such a connection, once you knew what you were looking for. It wouldn't need to be 100 percent correlation, naturally, nothing ever is indeed, such a figure would in itself be suspect. All that was required was a correlation well above chance . . .

Martin felt his mouth dry, his heart pounding: the Eureka feeling, that he had never thought to feel again. That these projected studies might give negative, or merely non-significant, results scarcely brushed the outer rim of his consciousness, so immersed was he now in designing the set-up for these tests. Obviously, it was going to involve some pretty drastic changes in the existing questionnaire, including substantial additions; and it would involve, too, the interviewing of not one person but two, in respect of each of the 64 subjects. In every case, not only the depressive himself, but the likely Parasite Person would have to be questioned in depth; and on top of this there would have to be call-backs on each of the fourteen subjects already interviewed. Instead of the original 64, a total of 128 interviews would now have to be undertaken: exactly doubling the original work-load.

For one moment, he panicked. Already, he was way behind schedule with the interviews, and now the prospect of actually *doubling* them . . . !

The panic passed, almost before it had properly made itself felt.

For was there not Ruth Ledbetter now, beavering away at the interviews with a speed and efficiency that almost took his breath away? Five she'd brought in yesterday, and four the day before, nearly all of them long and very thorough, full of the sort of intimate revelations which only a top-class interviewer knows how to elicit.

Nine in two days—nearly thirty a week! Long before that deadline in May, the whole lot would be in the bag!

He'd never known such a marvellous interviewer—never! And any moment now, she'd be along with today's supply!

CHAPTER 17

"So poor old Parsons is gone at last!" said Miss Crane, indicating with a well-shaped but unvarnished finger-nail the relevant spot in the Births, Marriages and Deaths page of the local paper. "Look. Albert Vincent Parsons, of 24 Lymington House —it must be him! Ninety-four—my goodness! I never realised he was *that* old. Why, he must have been gone seventy already when I first came . . . !"

Somewhat blank looks were all she got in the way of response from the other occupants of the staff-room, and she had to explain:

"You wouldn't remember him, of course, you young ones, but he was the caretaker here for—oh—something like fifty years it must have been. He retired soon after I got here, I remember the Presentation, and half the school in tears, though by all accounts he must have been a holy terror. He used to hook the children off the Governors' Lawn by their coat belts with a window-pole, and then chase them with it all the way to the playground steps, yelling frightful threats at them. The Governors' Lawn," she explained patiently, for the sake of those who still looked blank, "was at the far end of the playground; you know, that muddy bit, where it says 'KEEP OFF THE GRASS.' Well, there used to be grass there once. And the children had to keep off it." She sighed. "I suppose Parsons was the last person left alive who actually knew how to stop kids doing things; and now he's dead, too! Ah well . . . !"

She sighed, laid down the paper, and began putting her books together for her next lesson. When she had gone, Helen, who had a free period ahead, idly picked up the paper to glance through while she finished her coffee.

Ninety-four! Quite a character, too, by the sound of it. Vaguely intrigued by what Gillian Crane had told them, Helen cast her eyes over the remaining few lines of the insertion, and was pleased to note that the cantankerous and colourful old man had at least had a good send-off. Not for him the lonely end usually experienced by those who outlive by so many years the allotted span; on the contrary he was "Deeply mourned by his son, his four surviving daughters, his nineteen grandchildren, his eleven great-grandchildren."

A good life. A full life. Helen found her eyes wandering idly down the rest of the column to see what sort of deaths the others had died, and at what sort of age.

"Peacefully, in his own home, after a long illness, Gordon White, aged 79, beloved husband of Maud . . ."

"After a long illness bravely borne, Doris, much loved sister of Gertie and Win, aged 83 . . ."

Yes, most of them seemed to be truly mourned by somebody or other. Most of them seemed to have had good long lives—and then, suddenly, Helen stiffened. If anyone else had been in the staff-room to notice it, they would have seen the paper shaking in her hand as she picked it up to look closer . . . to see if she hadn't, somehow, misread the small print. . . .

No, there it was, just as it had first caught her eye:

"Suddenly, at his own home, Mr. Clive Willis, of 17 Whitbread Dranslord aged 59 . . ."

There could be no mistake. Only yesterday—only last night —she had been typing this very name, this very address, at the head of one of Martin's new interviews. One of Ruth's, rather, this Ruth Ledbetter, who had taken over (Martin had explained) from the incompetent Walter as his chief assistant. It had been a long interview, Helen remembered, and quite extraordinarily interesting: after typing it, together with two or

three others equally good, she had agreed with Martin whole-
heartedly that this Ruth girl, despite her off-putting manner,
was proving herself an absolutely top-class interviewer, with a
real gift for putting her subjects at their ease and extracting
from them the most surprisingly detailed and intimate information. This Clive Willis, she recalled, had been particularly
revealing about his relationship with his wife, who had been
"wonderful" to him ever since the depression had first struck:

"Such a marvellous woman . . . so patient . . . I don't
know how she puts up with me, I really don't . . . I'm
such poor company these days . . . And then she has her
job, as well . . . yes, a part-time job every afternoon, and
the pity of it is that it's the afternoons that are just the
times when I begin to feel a bit better . . . you know, I
can sort of get myself going . . . and that's just the time
when she's not there to see it! A shame, really . . ."

And now he was dead! Helen felt the shock almost as if she
had actually known him, after having typed out so many of his
inmost thoughts.

How sad! How very sad! And only fifty-nine, too.

"Suddenly," it said: was this a euphemism for suicide? With
depression this was a small but ever-present risk. If only one
was able to *do* something for these people, instead of just interviewing them; but of course that wasn't what Martin's research
was all about. It was a shame.

By now, the shock was subsiding slightly, but it left her,
somehow, with a compulsive need to read to the end of column, as if the list of unfamiliar names would be in some way
reassuring.

But that first shock was as nothing to the second.

"Mrs. Claire Huntingdon, of Tewkesbury Avenue aged
44 . . ."

This, too, she had typed, word for word, this very morning!

It couldn't be true! It *couldn't!* She must be dreaming! She must be hallucinating!

Yes, that was it. The shock of that first item must be causing her to hallucinate a second, similar one. Shock could do that sort of thing to you, she knew, though it was a bit disconcerting to discover that she, Helen, so sane and well-balanced, could be susceptible to such aberrations, even if only for a second or two.

She closed her eyes for a few moments, confident that when she opened them again, the item would be gone.

But it wasn't gone.

"Mrs. Claire Huntingdon, of Tewkesbury Avenue . . ."

It was impossible. It couldn't be happening.

But it was happening.

She must think, think. Putting her head in her hands, Helen tried to conceive of some credible explanation, because, of course, there must *be* one. The only answer she could come up with was, once again, the rather unsatisfying one that it was something inside her head that was running amok, and not the world outside. Since she wasn't hallucinating the newspaper item—she had looked at it too many times to doubt its reality any more—then maybe it was her memory that had gone haywire? Maybe the shock had affected her in such a way that she *thought* she'd typed that name and address this morning when in fact she hadn't . . . a sort of *déjà-vu* phenomenon . . . ?

Luckily, the phone was free—well, it would be, with everyone else at lessons—and luckily, too, there was no one passing along the passage outside the booth and overhearing, possibly, the bizarre conversation that was about to take place.

"Martin Lockwood speaking. Who is it?"

His voice, so cold, so peremptory, almost left her speechless; but then, quickly, she reminded herself how preoccupied he was with his work these days; and how marvellous it was that he should be so. She should be glad, not affronted, that he was so absorbed in what he was doing that interruptions were intolerable to him.

"Darling—it's me. I'm terribly sorry to interrupt you, but it won't take a moment. That interview I typed this morning—the one right on top of the pile? What exactly was the woman's name . . . ? And her address . . . ?"

"Well—for God's sake!" Martin's voice was, if anything, more irritable than ever. "Do you have to bother me about it *now*? Can't it wait till you get home?"

There was a pause; and during the brief silence Helen became aware of sudden tension coming at her down the line, a mounting wariness.

"What *is* all this, anyway?" he barked. "Why do you want to know?"

"Because she's dead: that's why," Helen snapped back, suddenly angry in her turn. "Her name's in the paper—in the Obituary column! 'Mrs. Claire Huntingdon, of 11 Tewkesbury Avenue . . .' It's right here, in front of me. I just want to check that it *is* the same name as on that interview. . . . *Please*, darling. . . . I mean, it's a bit scarey. . . . It seems so awful. . . ."

She was talking into empty air. He had moved away from the telephone, she could tell, and was now, presumably, looking for the interview in question. Not that it needed looking for—it was right on top of the pile, beside the typewriter.

She waited. She went on waiting. It was a mercy, at least, that everyone else was still in class; as soon as the lunch bell went it would be bedlam, with queues of people waiting outside the telephone booth, and further conversation would be impossible.

She looked at her watch. It was all right; a full ten minutes still to go; ten minutes of privacy to thrash the thing out quietly.

Nine minutes . . . eight minutes . . . What was he *doing* all this time? Had he mislaid the interview somehow, heedlessly piling his new exciting pages of typescript here, there and everywhere, obliterating everything else under the unstoppable products of his inspiration? Beyond the telephone booth, the faint, muted hum of a well-ordered school at lesson-time just reached her, while down the telephone wire, from her far-off flat, the silence was absolute.

Five minutes had passed; six. Her ear, pressed to the receiver, throbbed with listening; her cheek ached with the pressure of the instrument against it.

"Bugger off!" suddenly snarled a loud and instantly recognisable voice, right into her ear. "Just bugger off, will you?" and forthwith the receiver was slammed down with a noise like crashing furniture.

So Ruth was there. Ruth-Bloody-Leadswinger, as Beatrice had so aptly named her. Helen stood for a moment, her ears singing, and her anxiety swiftly being replaced by sheer fury.

That bloody girl! She had a devil in her, she really had! She was nothing but trouble! Trouble, trouble, trouble, wherever she went, and the insolence of her was beyond endurance! Why in Heaven's name must Martin choose *her*, of all people, to be his research assistant, his replacement for Walter . . . ?

Because she was so bloody good; that's why. This was the answer, and it was irrefutable. Helen made a big effort to calm herself, to see the thing in proportion.

Here was Martin, the man she loved, the man who was to all intents and purposes her husband, desperately behind with his work, desperately worried about it; and now, out of the blue, as if dropped by Heaven itself, comes this superbly competent and marvellously enthusiastic assistant, who was not only taking off Martin's shoulders a huge and gruelling load of work, but also seemed in some way to have inspired in him a quite extraordinary burst of creativity such as he had been awaiting in vain for months and years. For there was no getting away from it—Helen forced herself to be absolutely honest about this—there was no getting away from the fact that Martin's sudden burst of creative euphoria had coincided just about exactly with Ruth's appearance on the scene; and for this incomparable service, by whatever means it had been achieved, the ill-mannered, coarse-spoken young woman must be forgiven *anything*.

Yes, *anything*. Helen felt pretty certain, in her own heart, that it was not sex that was the driving force in this sudden, headlong partnership between her lover and this peculiar girl; but even if it had been, Helen told herself stoutly, it would have been worth it. To see her beloved Martin happy at last, inspired at last, succeeding at last in his long-frustrated ambitions—for this, there was no price too high to pay. No price at all.

CHAPTER 18

"Coincidence, darling," Martin assured her off-handedly when she finally succeeded in making him look for himself at the announcements in the paper, and to compare them with the names and addresses on the interviews. "These things are bound to happen sometimes, you know. After all, depressives *do* commit suicide quite often. It's one of the hazards of our job."

Not "quite often." From her intensive apprenticeship to the subject on Martin's behalf, and her consequent wide reading, Helen knew very well that depressives, although somewhat more prone to suicide than the general population, were not all that likely to meet their deaths in this way. That two out of nine of Ruth's subjects to date should have died within a week seemed to Helen to be quite beyond the bounds of coincidence. Besides . . .

"Martin—*please!* There's nothing in the notices to say that they *were* suicides, either of them. 'Suddenly' doesn't *have* to be a euphemism. Besides—two out of nine in a single week! It *can't* be coincidence! The chances against it . . ."

"Look, darling, you're ever such a clever girl, we all know that. You've got an I.Q. way up in the stratosphere, I don't doubt it. But do you, actually, sweetie, know anything *about* the laws of Chance and Probability? It's a highly specialised field, you know; you have to be something of a mathematician before you can even begin to grasp it. I don't claim to be an expert myself, but I *did* do a bit of Probability Theory as part of my degree course—which you, my sweetheart, didn't—let's face it! And I can tell you this much: coincidences *have* to happen sometimes. They mathematically have to. It would be if there *weren't* any coincidences any more that we'd have to start wondering what had gone wrong with the universe!

"Look at it this way. Suppose, instead of nine interviews, Ruth had done a million. *Then* would you think it such a frantic coincidence if out of these million, two should appear in the death column this week? Would you?"

"Of course not, Not out of a *million*. But . . ."

"But nothing, lovey! Don't you see? These two coincidences have got to come *somewhere* among the million, if they are to be there at all, and every single place they could come is just as unlikely as any other place! Being in the first nine is no more unlikely than being in any other particular place! If you think of these nine interviews as being the first nine out of a million— and if Ruth *was* going to do a million then they *would* be— then the 'coincidence' problem just doesn't arise. Wherever they were in the million, it would be just as much a 'coincidence' that they should be just exactly there. Don't you see?"

That there was a huge, jumbo-sized fallacy somewhere in this argument, Helen was absolutely certain. But exactly where the fallacy lay, and how it could be countered, she did not know. He was blinding her with mathematics; that much was clear to her. But the question still remained, was he blinding himself as well?

Full of unease, she glanced warily up at him, and found herself looking into his shining, triumphant face, all lit up with success and with fulfilment.

How could she destroy such radiance, for the sake of a mere logical fallacy? Why not bask in it? Enjoy it? Revel in the fact that the hopes and struggles of the last months had borne fruit at last?

And yet . . . and yet. Two people had died. Not old people, either; one of them was only forty-four. It *wasn't* coincidence, it *couldn't* be, not all the mathematicians in the world were going to convince her to the contrary.

Something weird, something sinister was afoot, it must be, and if she, Helen, took no action now, it would be on her conscience for the rest of her days.

"Look, darling," she began, with infinite caution, and attempting to approach the question from another, totally non-mathematical direction: "This girl—this Ruth Ledbetter. I know she's a marvellous interviewer and all that, but do you actually know anything *about* her? I mean . . ."

"I know what you mean!" Martin's handsome face was flushed, his eyes blazing, and yet, despite these overt signs of anger, Helen had the momentary impression that he was relieved; relieved that he had an excuse, now, to quarrel with her, thus bringing rational argument to an end.

"I know what you mean. You mean you're jealous of her," he accused. "You're jealous of her helping me so efficiently—of being so damn good at the job! Of—well—of *inspiring* me, as nobody has ever inspired me before . . . !"

Was she jealous? Was there something in these accusations? If Martin had stopped there, Helen might have been prepared to admit to a grain of truth in what he was saying. But he did not stop there.

"You've had it in for her right from the start!" he blustered. "You've been absolutely beastly to her, from the very beginning!"

This was too much! After all Helen's tolerance and forebearance, her unfailing civility in the face of the girl's insolence, her outrageous manners, her cool assumption that she could walk into Helen's flat just whenever she chose, and monopolise the attention of Helen's lover for just as long as she liked! After all this, to be told . . . !

"Well, I like that!" Helen flared back. "*I'm* beastly to *her!* I really do like that! What about the way *she* treats *me?* What about her telling me this morning to 'Bugger off!' when I telephone my own flat . . . ? 'Just bugger off, will you?' she said . . . !"

Now that he had got her angry, Martin seemed to be in some way satisfied. His own anger evaporated.

"Oh, now, come off it, darling," he said placatingly. "That isn't what she said at all. You must have misheard her. She must have said 'Must be running off now'—something like that. You know how it is on the telephone. And your school telephone particularly—all that row outside in the corridor all the time . . . !"

He paused; and when Helen said nothing, he allowed a self-pitying note to creep into his voice:

"I do wish, darling, that you'd try to see it a bit from my point of view. Okay, so Ruth hasn't got the most polished manners in the world, but after all, she's only young, and you know what the young are like these days—you've often re-marked on it yourself, you know you have, when you've had a rotten day at school! But those are just superficialities—let's try, if we can, to keep to essentials. And the essential thing here is that I need her—I absolutely *need* her—for my work. Do try to understand, Helen, that this is something *important* to me. It's the chance of a lifetime! I've never had such a fantastically brilliant and hard-working interviewer, never! It's like magic, the way she gets the buggers talking—really reveal-ing themselves—their real, deep feelings, that they've never revealed to anyone before! It's incredible, what she gets out of them! I've never known anything like it!"

Neither had Helen. She had typed quite a few of Ruth's in-terviews by now, and even before the shock of this morning's discoveries, she had begun to feel uneasy about them, though it was difficult to know just what to put her finger on. There was the right and to-be-expected proportion of dull, inartic-ulate sort of people that you get in any survey, with nothing much to say for themselves, and with no new light to throw on anything.

But the ones who were articulate—they were *so* articulate! So full of startling revelations, of bizarre and striking turns of phrase: "Good quotes" as Martin exultantly termed them, he was absolutely delighted; and it was this delight, so heartfelt, so unclouded, that had caused Helen so far to keep her doubts to herself.

Two people have died. The words would not leave her alone, hammering away inside her skull in and out of season. Two of Martin's research subjects, for the interviewing of whom he, Martin, was strictly responsible, even though he might choose to delegate the job—two of them were dead. He, and no one else, would be held responsible—and rightly—for any malpractice that might be going on.

Reluctant though she was to re-open the recent quarrel—already Martin seemed to have got over his burst of ill-temper and was humming contentedly as he moved around the room assembling glasses, bottles, ice, for their usual evening drinks—Helen knew she must speak. It could not be left like this. It just could not.

"Darling," she began—and already her voice was so full of nervousness, reluctance and downright fear that the innocent little word stopped him in his tracks. He stood, tray of glassware in hand, as if in front of a camera. "Darling, I don't want to upset anything, I'm as thrilled as you are that it's all going so well—that Ruth's getting you such marvellous interviews. But had you thought at all—I mean, it's quite usual in these surveys, isn't it?—had you thought of doing the odd call-back on the people she's interviewed? Just as a matter of routine, I mean, the way they do it in Market Research—the supervisor calls back on, say, one in ten of the addresses just to . . ."

"Just to what?"

Martin's voice was so cold, so menacing, that Helen found herself shrinking back into her corner of the settee, unable to look at him.

"And since when have I needed a little O-level schoolmarm to explain to me the proper way to run a survey? I might remind you, Helen my dear, that I was working on public opinion surveys—including Market Research projects—when you were hardly out of primary school! When I need you to in-struct me on the elementary principles of this branch of Social Science I shall ask you, thank you very much!"

Helen physically shrivelled under the snub. Her blonde hair, golden in the lamplight, fell like a curtain across her white face as she stared down into her lap, fingers lacing and interlacing, her knuckles whitening.

But she would not give in.

"I think, Martin," she said quietly, "that you ought to do a call-back at those two addresses where the people died. I don't care how much I'm interfering, I don't care how furious you are. But I think you ought. There. I've said it. And you've heard me say it. I won't say it again."

For one moment, she thought he was going to hit her; but when, cautiously, she raised her head just enough to see through the pale mist of her hair, she saw that he had not moved. He was still standing exactly as before, and though the glasses were not even rattling on the tray, and though his voice, when he spoke, was as icily sarcastic as ever, she knew, without knowing how she knew, that somehow she had fright-ened him.

"A call-back at the addresses of the two people who died,"— he repeated her own words back to her, exactly as in a depth-interview. "And what, precisely, are you expecting that that will reveal? In plain words, what are you accusing Ruth of? Murder? Manslaughter? You see her as some sort of female Ripper? Or what?"

CHAPTER 19

Mr. Maynard (Maths) was looking really happy for the first time in living memory. His crossword puzzle had been laid aside unfinished, his slightly frog-like face, usually furrowed with worry and boredom, was puckered now with a quite different set of lines, criss-cross wrinkles of pleasure and excitement: and—a quite unheard-of phenomenon this, reducing the rest of the staff-room to awed silence—he was talking, nineteen to the dozen.

The subject of his discourse was billiard-balls. Not your common-or-garden billiard-balls, fit only for playing billiards with, but *one million* billiard-balls, of which just two were black, and all the rest white. Supposing, Helen had asked him, really wanting to know the answer (and this in itself is a rare enough occurrence in any teacher's day) supposing you had all these billiard-balls mixed up at random in a gigantic sack, and supposing you put your hand in and pulled out nine of them—what were the chances of the two black ones being among them?

Helen had given much thought to the mode of presenting her problem and had decided to dehumanise it in this way in order to deceive the assembled gossips into thinking that she was talking about something genuinely boring, and thus throw them off the scent.

It proved to have been a very good idea. Mr. Maynard was loving it.

"Just to make the arithmetic simpler," he suggested, a little apologetically, "shall we say that it's *ten* that you manage to gather into your hand rather than nine? The *principle* will be the same; but of course if the actual figure nine is important to your purposes, then I could easily . . ."

Helen shook her head, hastily. Making the arithmetic simpler seemed to her an entirely good idea.

"Right. Now, let's see . . ." Mr. Maynard gave a little wriggle of satisfaction as the calculation took shape in his mind. "Ten billiard-balls out of a million, yes? So first let us divide this million into sets of ten, shall we? Of which this first set, the one you pick out, is just one, yes? All together, there will be 100,000 such sets in the sack—are you with me?"

Helen nodded. He was making it far clearer than Martin had done.

"And so it follows," continued her eager instructor, "that the chances of any particular one of these black balls being in any particular one of these sets of ten will be 100,000 to one against. Right? That's just for *one* of the black balls. Now, here you must listen carefully, because many people—even quite intelligent people—are inclined to imagine in a case like this that the chances against *two* balls being in the given set are merely double the chances against one—a mere 200,000, in fact, in our present case.

"But, dear me, how they deceive themselves, these people! The figure doesn't merely have to be *doubled* in this kind of case: it has to be *squared!*" He looked at Helen wide-eyed, waiting for her to be impressed: which indeed she was, though a little bemused. Kindly, he translated for her.

"One hundred thousand *squared*," he said, "comes to ten thousand million. So those are your odds, my dear. Ten thousand million against."

He laughed his dry, little-used laugh.

"And so if someone is trying to persuade you to gamble on these sort of odds, my dear, then you must say No to him, immediately! You must indeed!"

Helen thanked him effusively for the trouble he had taken over his explanation, promised faithfully to heed his very pru-

dent advice, and made her way back across the staff-room to
her usual seat, Mr. Maynard's gaze following her yearningly as
she went. It wasn't often that anyone asked him anything of
the smallest interest or importance, and it had quite made his
day.

"So what was all *that* in aid of?" Wendy whispered loudly,
leaning across an intervening figure trying to add up the morning's milk-money. "Are you seeking the way to his heart
through rows of noughts? You could be right, at that!"

She giggled, still tilted at this awkward angle waiting for
Helen to giggle too, and say something amusing; but Helen
just smiled vaguely, and shook her head, thus bringing the conversation to an end. She very much wanted it to be at an end
because she well knew that a bit of skilful probing by Wendy
would soon break down her defences. Also, it seemed a bit
hard on the milk-calculator to be leaned across like this; rather
rude, really, since the poor woman neither wished nor was
being invited to take part in the somewhat idiotic conversation.

Helen was finding it hard to concentrate this morning on
anything. It was Thursday, her half-day, and the free afternoon
loomed ahead like a black cloud because of the awful thing she
was going to have to do.

The possibility of coincidence could be ruled out. She hadn't
really needed Mr. Maynard to spell out to her that there was a
fallacy in Martin's reasoning, but all the same it had been a
help, somehow, to consult him. With his kind, weary blue eyes
fixed on her earnestly, his dry voice setting out the calculations
so precisely, she had been able to feel that she was not coming
to her dreadful decision totally and entirely on her own.

It was the only possible decision, she had known this ever
since last night. *Someone* had to call back at those two fatal
addresses, and since Martin refused to, then she, Helen, must
do it.

The treachery of it seemed awful: but the treachery of *not*
doing it was even worse. How could she stand by and allow

Martin to walk, in blind, pig-headed innocence, into some bizarre and incomprehensible trap?

In the suburb where Mrs. Claire Huntingdon had met her death, daffodils were already thrusting up out of the dark earth, and crocuses were massing in purple and gold alongside the trim lawns. February was over at last, and spring was everywhere. Helen felt the warmth of the sun, for the first time in many months, through her thick winter coat, and the suddenness of the change was overwhelming.

Every year it was the same. Every year through the long dark days you know perfectly well that spring *will* come, and summer too. There they are, on the calendar, plain as a clock-face. You even fill in dates in your diary, on the absolute assumption that these dates will come; that April will be followed by May, that there will *be* such a month as June, and that on the 19th of July the summer term will end. You don't question the arrival of these dates, not for one single moment. Nobody does.

But all the time, something deep inside you doesn't believe a word of it. Something in you is totally adjusted to winter, and only to winter; believes only in winter, and is shocked rigid, year after year, when the first spring day is suddenly upon you.

And this year, for Helen, it had to be today of all days when this happened. She had enough on her mind already, without this disorientation caused by the tilting of the earth in its orbit. She walked along Tewkesbury Avenue in a sort of daze, her body ecstatic with the reviving sun, her mind dark with fears.

Number Eleven was pretty much like all the other houses in the road; the front garden was as neat, the bulbs as far advanced. The only difference was that at two of the upstairs windows the blinds were drawn.

And it was only now that Helen realised, quite suddenly, how impossible was this venture on which she had embarked.

Because you couldn't *do* this sort of thing. You just couldn't.

How could you, a complete stranger, walk calmly into a house of mourning, and start asking intrusive questions about how the lost loved one had spent her last days—perhaps even hours —on earth? Had she had a visitor just before she died— someone she'd never met before, armed with a notebook, asking all sorts of personal questions? How had the deceased answered? Was there any kind of an angry scene? And if you have no evidence that any of this happened, have you, on the other hand, any evidence that it didn't . . . ?

It was unthinkable. Helen looked at the quiet house, pictured the grief-stricken family inside—quite a young family, probably, since Claire Huntingdon had only been forty-four. She pictured a shattered young teenager opening the door to her, the eldest girl, eyes red with weeping for her mother . . . and she turned and almost ran down the road, back the way she had come, ashamed, now, of ever having contemplated such an intrusion. No wonder she had dreaded the expedition so, had had her whole morning darkened by it. Her heart had been warning her all along that this was a thing she simply could not do.

Still the sun shone. The spring afternoon was yet young. Surely there was *something* she could do, other than slink home defeated and let matters take their course, dragging Martin with them, to the ruination, perhaps, of his whole career?

At the bus stop, she stood still, and forced herself to think.

If only she knew where Ruth lived! Then the thing to do would be to go straight there, now, and tackle the girl head-on, by-passing altogether Martin's all-too-predictable views on such a course of action. Alone together, just the two of them, free of Martin's defensive interruptions on Ruth's behalf, Helen had little doubt that she would be able to win the girl's confidence, at least sufficiently to get *some* sort of idea of what it was she was up to. Her years of experience with schoolgirls had taught her that if you can once get a girl by herself, and talk to her quietly, on a one-to-one basis, it is almost always possible to come to terms with even the most determined of troublemakers. That the method would work with Ruth Ledbetter she had little doubt—after all, the girl was only nineteen, not much more than a schoolgirl—but what use was this if she didn't know where to find her? Whether Martin had deliberately concealed Ruth's address, or whether (and this would be typical of him) he'd never bothered to find it out in the first place, the result was the same: checkmate.

Who else might know it? There were no mutual friends, so far as Helen knew. Unless, of course, you counted Walter: but he, according to Martin, was so monumentally useless at absolutely everything that he hardly seemed worth bothering about: and in any case, she didn't know where he lived, either.

It all looked pretty hopeless.

But wait! It suddenly occurred to her that there *was* a mutual friend—a mutual enemy, rather, but none the worse for that, when it came to collecting scurrilous information about someone.

Beatrice. Only a few mornings ago, Beatrice had rung up in a state of great indignation about Ruth, complaining, in no uncertain terms, of the girl's insolence and bad manners.

Why not go and talk to Beatrice? Right now, while she had the whole free afternoon ahead of her? It could well be that in the course of her altercation with Ruth, Beatrice might have picked up any number of miscellaneous facts about her unwelcome visitor which she would be only too happy to divulge to a sympathetic listener.

The fact that Beatrice was the injured wife and she, Helen, the scarlet woman, seemed at the moment to be of little consequence. Curiosity is one of the strongest of all human emotions—though strangely neglected by politicians and economists, who fondly imagine that greed is the only vice worth exploiting—and Helen had little doubt of her welcome at Number 16 Hadley Gardens if she came around with so fascinating a mystery as this to discuss.

She had rung the bell twice before she made herself face the fact that Beatrice must be out. Since Martin had left her, Beatrice had had chimes installed, and as she listened to them tinkling coyly for the second time, Helen could not help reflecting, with a certain satisfaction, on how much Martin would have hated this sort of thing. Free of his rigidly uplifting presence, Beatrice was fast turning into the person she really was, chimes and all. No doubt there would be plaster gnomes on the front lawn before the season was much further advanced, Helen smugly surmised. Not that she had anything against plaster gnomes herself; they could look quite jolly, sometimes; but she had lived with Martin long enough by now to see them through his eyes, and to know that they were a Bad Thing, and that only the most despicable people went in for them. Signs of despicableness in Beatrice still stirred in her a certain gratification, though this was a habit she should be getting out of by now. Particularly if she was going to treat Beatrice as a confidante every time her life with Martin ran into a rough patch such as this. . . .

Perhaps Beatrice was out at the back, gardening? This first day of real spring always brought people out into their gardens, madly doing *something*, even if only damage, to the nascent growth.

She set off round to the back, passing the dustbins—new ones, one scarlet and one sky-blue. Again, not Martin's taste, but they did brighten up the dank, sunless passageway, no doubt about it.

There was no sign of Beatrice in the garden; nor, indeed, any signs of gardening in progress. No tools, no wheelbarrows intruded their note of human restlessness into the quiet cycle of growth that was going on from fence to fence in all directions.

Was it worth waiting for Beatrice to come home? But she might be out for all the rest of the day—or even be away altogether, on holiday or something? Impelled by a vague curiosity, Helen rounded the far corner of the house and stood on tiptoe to look in through the kitchen window.

At first, she could see almost nothing, so accustomed were her eyes to the sharp radiance outdoors; but gradually her vision cleared, and she could see that the kitchen was indeed currently in use; it didn't look at all like the kitchen of someone who has packed up and gone on holiday. A half-empty bottle of milk, still looking quite fresh, stood on top of the refrigerator; and on the draining-board, in a saucepan of cold water, some freshly-peeled potatoes were awaiting the time when it might be convenient for someone to cook them. You shouldn't do this, of course, it's bad for potatoes to be left to soak like this, it takes away all the flavour: but that was typical Beatrice for you. The kitchen table had on it a pale blue plastic cloth adorned with smudgy pictures of knives and forks and lobsters and things. At the moment, it was covered with crumbs, and at one end lay the remains of a salad lunch, beetroot and bits of lettuce, together with an open packet of sliced bread and a dish of butter without a lid. In the midst of all this sat the Lockwoods' tabby cat, licking itself contentedly, as it had no doubt been licking its fill of the butter. The way Beatrice would never discipline that cat had been one of Martin's early grievances, Helen remembered; and in those days, in the heyday of her self-imposed mission to succeed triumphantly in every area where Beatrice failed, this could have presented quite a problem, for she was no more capable of disciplining a cat that has made up its mind what it wants to do, than anyone else is. Mercifully, however, this grievance of Martin's had been followed up almost immediately by one concerning Beatrice's insistence on keeping a cat at all; and here Helen had been able effortlessly to excel. Nothing is easier than not keeping a cat, especially if you live on the third floor, whereas disciplining one is very nearly beyond the wit of humankind.

The place was very quiet. The cat went on licking itself, the sun moved inch by inch towards the butter, which would soon be squashy and yellow, its own special way of celebrating the return of spring. In the far corner, above the sink, a tap dripped steadily, needing a new washer. This was another thing that Martin wouldn't have been able to stand. The mincer, too, with scraps of raw meat still adhering, standing on *today's* newspaper. That was something else that he had a thing about, using today's paper for household tasks; never mind the cat having had a go at the mincer, as well.

The place was untidy, certainly; even neglected, in a way; but not in the way that a place is neglected when the owner is actually away. This was current, day-to-day neglect, mere sloppiness, a general Beatrice-way of doing things. Soon, the remains of supper would be joining the remains of lunch, and no doubt Beatrice would get around to washing up as soon as there was nowhere to put anything down except on the floor.

And then she saw them. Sticking out from under the tablecloth, with one down-at-heel slipper off, the other still covering the laddered toes of her stocking—Beatrice's feet. You could have thought they were dummies, a stage-set, except that you knew they couldn't be.

Helen's first impulse was to scream. Her second, to smash the window with the nearest hard implement—her fist, if necessary—and scramble to the rescue.

Rescue? But it was too late for rescue. Those feet . . . so still . . . so lifeless . . . so unresponsive to the sharp little sound of terror which Helen knew she had made. . . . Beatrice must be already dead.

Ruth's *third* victim? For hadn't that been an "interview" of sorts that Beatrice had been describing in such trenchant terms just before the phone went dead . . . ?

Dead. Helen shuddered, and with the sun still beating on her back she felt icy cold.

Was that the precise moment when it had happened? Had she, Helen, actually been present at the murder, albeit on the end of a telephone? And had just shrugged her shoulders, assuming a fault on the line, and bothered no more about it?

There was a roaring in her ears now, she felt as if she was choking, but Helen forced herself to batten down the panic, to pull herself out of shock, and to try to think rationally.

The thing she was imagining was impossible. Whatever had happened, it couldn't have happened all those days ago. Look at those remains of an obviously recent meal; look at the opened bottle of milk, not yet curdled and yellow. And what about the contented cat, washing itself? Surely no cat would sit licking itself in this leisurely way if its mistress had been lying dead for a week less than a yard away?

Or would it? Helen knew so little about cats. Were they truly attached to their owners, other than by cupboard-love? Did they *care*?

And even if they did care, would they necessarily show their caring by not getting on the table to wash themselves, by refraining from licking the butter . . . ?

"Beet! It's all right, Beet, you can come out now!"

The voice, screeching from an upstairs window, startled Helen almost out of her senses, though even in that first moment of shock she still managed to recognise it: it was the voice of the Pocock woman from across the road, Beatrice's bosom friend, and Martin's No. 1 *bête noire*. The black, shining scrolls of hair bobbed and quivered above the window-ledge up there, and the face was so red with excitement and glee that the over-rouged cheeks looked almost natural.

"It's *all right*, Beet!" the voice howled again; and then, full of explanatory gusto:

"It's not *her*, Beet, this time! It's only *her!*"

CHAPTER 20

At the second exhortation—"You can come out now, Beet"—
the feet protruding from beneath the table began, reassuringly,
to stir, one of them groping ineffectually for the lost slipper,
the other withdrawing itself from sight as its owner, heaving
herself around in her cramped quarters like a beached sea-
monster, prepared to emerge into the light of day. The crisis
was over, evidently. Beatrice, sheepish and dishevelled, but no
longer scared, crawled out from her hiding place, and with
much cracking of joints scrambled up to a standing position.
She turned to face Helen, blinking into the sunlight.

"Oh. It's you," she said, still a bit dazed; and then, vaguely
hospitable: "Do come in."

Through the window? Or round to the back door? Beatrice,
still blinking, seemed oblivious of the problem: just looked at
Helen expectantly, waiting for her to materialise indoors. But
at this point the problem was solved by Marjorie Pocock bursting in at the back door agog with neighbourly joy at the prospect of something happening, but not to her.

"It's *her!*" she exulted, for the third time, though on this oc-
casion lowering her voice a little in deference to Helen's prox-
imity, "Martin's fancy piece! Do you want to let her in?"

By now, Beatrice had dusted herself down, had both her
slippers on, and was already padding to the back door.

"Oh, there you are," she said, amiably enough, as Helen appeared round the corner of the house. "It's funny you should
turn up just now, we were just talking about you."

Since the two of them must have talked of little else for the best part of eighteen months, the coincidence was not startling; but Helen took the remark as it was meant, as a sort of "come-and-join-the-club" invitation, and soon the three of them were seated round the kitchen table drinking mugs of inordinately strong tea. The crumbs were still there, and the liquifying butter, but the cat had made itself scarce, doubtless calculating, with that universal feline wisdom, that visitors nearly always prove a threat, bringing with them fearsomely uncat standards of hygiene with which to intimidate your normally easy-going owner. "Down, puss!" she will cry, in tones of wholly factitious horror, and will even push you off the table quite sharply, in that nasty, showing-off way, trying to make them believe that this was what she normally did.

Really, humans! What traitors they became to your cosy working relationship whenever there was another human around.

Helen sipped the nasty and none-too-hot tea, accepted a slice of swiss roll out of a cardboard packet, and wished heartily that Marjorie would go so that she could have her private conversation with Beatrice about Ruth Ledbetter. That was what she had come for, and she did not want to waste time on social chit-chat.

She need not have worried. Marjorie did not want to waste time on social chit-chat either, she plunged straight in.

"You must be wondering," she said to Helen, before even biting into her swiss roll, "why Beet was under the table when you arrived? A bit funny, didn't you think?"

"Well, a bit," Helen agreed cautiously, adding "But of course it's none of my business . . ."

"*None of your business?*" shrieked Marjorie, slapping her mug of tea down so hard that it slopped over on to the (luckily) plastic table-cloth. "But *of course* it's your business! *I'd* damn well think it was *my* business if my partner's Ex was hiding under the kitchen table when I called! But, of course, she never would be . . . she's not like that. . . ."

She sighed, as if having a rival in love who doesn't hide

under tables at your approach was one of life's minor depriva-
tions. Then, cheering up, she continued:

"She wasn't hiding from *you*, Helen, don't think that you
weren't, were you, Beet?" and Beatrice, her mouth full of swiss
roll, nodded emphatic assent. "She was hiding from that *other*
one. The Leadswinger one. Weren't you, Beet? The one who
keeps coming round persecuting her. A dozen times she's been
here, I should think. Tell her about it, Beet. Go on."

Beatrice nodded, swallowed the remainder of her mouthful,
and took up the narrative.

"That's right. Well, perhaps not a *dozen* times, but at least
twice. I told you, Helen, don't you remember, how rude she
was that time? Badgering me about Martin's work, just as if *I*
knew anything about it, why should I? His *work!*—that always
makes me laugh, anything to do with Martin working! I'm
sorry, Helen, but it does. I've known him longer than you
have.

"So anyway, about this ghastly girl. I got rid of her that
time, and I thought that was the end of it. But not two days
later—something like that, anyway—there she was again. The
nerve of it! Crack of dawn it was that time, I wasn't even up.
So that's when I phoned you, Helen. Enough is enough, I
thought—and I think that scared her a bit, hearing me telling
you all about it on the upstairs extension. She maybe thought
Martin was listening, I don't know, anyway, she cut us off half
through a sentence, and when I ran downstairs to ask what the
hell, she'd gone. Since then I haven't let her in, and I think
she'd given up now. Thank goodness. Long time no see, that's
what I'm praying for."

In all this, there wasn't much that Helen didn't already
know, and the questions she could think of asking didn't
elucidate much more. No, Beatrice *didn't* know the girl's address, how should she? Nor anything at all about her background, it wasn't quite that sort of a friendly chat, was it? Just
a lot of nosey-parkering about Martin, and the stuff he was
working on just now. . . .

And talking of Martin's stuff, she continued, somewhat tartly, what about all that junk of his in the back bedroom? When was he coming to move it? Because now that she wasn't going to get a bloody penny from him, just the house, she was going to have to think about making an income from it, wasn't she? She was planning to take in lodgers; she could make thirty pounds a week, easily, out of that back bedroom once Martin's clobber was out of it.

"Forty pounds," interposed Marjorie, who liked to see dissension escalating.

"And so," reasoned Beatrice, "every week he doesn't take that bloody stuff away is costing me thirty pounds."

"Forty pounds," said Marjorie.

"And so in fact," continued Beatrice, "If you work it out, he owes me ninety pounds already—"

Hastily, before Marjorie could work out what three forties were, Helen intervened.

"I'm sorry, Beatrice, I really am. I do see what a nuisance it is for you; but the point is, my flat isn't very large, and I've already taken quite a few of his things. The desk, for instance, and that nest of tables. It isn't as if we *need* any more furniture."

Rivalry, temporarily in abeyance, was astir again. As much as they had once fought to possess Martin's person, so did they now fight not to possess his filing-cabinets, his overflowing cardboard boxes, his mounds of obsolete papers pertaining to long-abandoned projects.

"You could have them put in store," suggested Helen, as she always suggested when the subject came up, "and send us the bill."

"*He* can have them put in store!" Beatrice snapped back, again in the identical words she had used on previous occasions. "They're *his* bloody things!"—and there, once again, the matter was allowed to rest. Since each of them felt herself to be the loser in this battle, it was never allowed to go on very long.

One way and another, it seemed about time for Helen to go. It was plain by now that Beatrice had nothing useful to contribute to the problem; also, for some minutes Helen had been aware of an increasing restlessness in her two companions. They were longing to get her out of the house so that they could start talking about her again; and taking pity on their impatience, and not wanting to outstay her welcome, Helen took her leave.

CHAPTER 21

Martin had been more perturbed by the two announcements in the Deaths Column than he had allowed Helen to see. He knew as well as she did that they couldn't be coincidence. But the reason for his anxiety was quite different from hers. Not for one moment did he suspect that Ruth might have somehow brought about the deaths of these two subjects; in fact he had reason to be certain that she had not. His fears related to a possibility quite other than this.

For he, too, in his student days had worked off-and-on as a part-time, partially-trained interviewer on various projects. He knew all the dodges, and this was one of them, it came in very useful in those surveys where a name and address was demanded as well as a complete set of answers. The reason for this demand was, of course, to enable check-ups to be made, and thus to deter the unscrupulous interviewer from doing the whole job in the comfort of his own armchair, making up answers out of his head.

A reasonable precaution, given the motley collection of people commonly employed as interviewers. But all the same, the system failed to take account of the ingenuity of some of the resourceful young people who got themselves employed, especially those of them who worked in teams, egging one another on, *Us* against *Them*. Whatever new obstacle *They* might set up to obviate cheating was taken as a challenge; and this particularly mean-spirited device of making you extract names and addresses from the people you accosted in the street, so that the supervisor could call back on one in ten of them (Helen

had been absolutely right, as usual) and check that the interview had in fact taken place—this device had stretched the
team's ingenuity to its exciting limit.

There had been various ploys; and this one, of picking
names out of the Deaths Column of the local paper had been
found to work surprisingly well, if used in moderation. No supervisor, finding herself (it was usually a her in this kind of
work) in a house of mourning, the subject of her inquiries
barely cold in his grave, would ever have the nerve to pursue
the matter: she would just fall over herself apologising, and
beat a hasty retreat.

Of course, you couldn't do too many like this, too consistently, or they'd begin to spot it. Ruth had been rather pushing her luck with as many as two out of nine. She was also
foolish in not realising that whereas in a vast, impersonal
Market Research Survey the chances were very small indeed
that any of the far-off staff at headquarters would be regular
readers of the local paper of your particular area, in this small-
scale survey of Martin's, in and around the campus, the
chances of this being the case were really quite high.

It was worrying. Not only worrying in itself, but it set you
wondering what else the naughty girl had been up to?

He tried to remember the other ploys they'd used; and as he
recalled them, one after another, from the golden, dare-devil
days, he could hardly refrain from smiling.

There was the "Fifth Girl" trick, for example. If you were
short of an "F 25 C" to complete your quota, you simply
looked through the Accommodation Vacant columns for "Fifth
Girl Wanted" for some communal flat or other; then copied
out that address (or rang up for it, if it was a box-number), invented a name at random, and then effortlessly filled in your
questionnaire, confident that if the supervisor *should* choose
this address as one of her one-in-tens, there would not be a single inhabitant who could say with certainty that there had or
had not been such a character temporarily in residence at such-
and-such a time: still less whether any among the myriad of re-

cent callers had or had not come from Market Investigations Ltd, or whatever.

Removal vans were good, too. The team kept each other posted about addresses outside which removal men had been observed carrying furniture. By the time the supervisor did her rounds, the newcomers would be safely installed, and naturally could not be expected to know anything much about the doings of their predecessors.

Of course, you couldn't do *all* your interviews like this; there was tacit agreement in the team that at least 50 per cent of your stuff had to be genuine. How else could there be any basis from which to calculate a plausible proportion of "Yeses" and "Nos" and "Don't knows" in the various categories? Besides, with any reasonably short, straightforward, and un-embarrassing questionnaire, it just wasn't worth the bother, it was easier and quicker to do the job properly. Where these dodges really came into their own was when you were landed with a long and complicated questionnaire to be administered by the Quota Method—so many C-class F's aged under 35, so many D-class M's of over 60, and so on, all of them to be accosted in the street with nothing better to go on than their appearance. Often, your guess could be quite absolutely wrong, and you could get quite desperate, picking on perky young girls who turned out to be over fifty, or down-and-out old wrecks who turned out to be headmasters of public schools or Peers of the Realm.

Though, of course, if you were *looking* for headmasters of public schools or Peers of the Realm (A-class males) to complete your quota, you could scour the streets for days and never come across a single one: and this was where "Round the World Cruises" came in so useful. You got hold of a glossy mag, full of gossip about who was just off for a 3-month yachting trip, and down his name would go, among your over-50 A's. The supervisor, patiently doing her rounds, would be confronted by the butler, who naturally could not be expected to know whether or not his master/mistress had recently been in-

terviewed in the street about toothpaste or whatever; and by
the time the said master/mistress returned from the jaunt, the
whole thing would be ancient history, sunk without trace.

What fun it had been! And how very nearly always it had
worked!

Somehow, it had never really seemed like cheating—more
like winning in a game of skill and daring against opponents
worthy of your mettle. Or, looked at in another way, it could
seem like the improvising of a set of labour-saving devices conducive to higher productivity per man-hour: an outcome for
which any sensible employer should surely be grateful?

And, of course, way back of it all, there was the solid, reassuring fact that 50 per cent of the stuff was genuine. The final
results couldn't be all that wildly out while this remained the
case and provided you calculated your proportions of "Yeses"
and "Nos" correctly. Usually, this was simply a matter of
doubling-up on your genuine figure in each category, even the
biggest moron could hardly get it wrong.

Also, working in a team helped. It was vitally important that
they should all of them get approximately the *same* proportions—if you turned in results more than 10 percent or so different from your colleagues, then you really *were* on the carpet,
and so the team took every precaution to ensure that this
should not occur.

And so, by and large, no real harm was done to anyone, certainly not to the advancement of human knowledge. Apart
from anything else, the topics being researched were usually of
such piddling idiocy—whether "Banana-flavoured ice-cream"
was a phrase more appealing to the consumer than "The ice-
cream with banana-flavouring": or whether blue pictures on the
packet sold detergent faster than pink ones—so that the concept of advancing (or, indeed, retarding) the march of science
was simply laughable.

And this was where the whole difference lay. This was why
Martin was both angry and worried. His concern about Ruth's

cheating in the very same ways that he himself had been accustomed to cheat wasn't just a matter of the pot calling the kettle black; for this was something quite, quite different. *This* survey was an important, scientific survey: it was *Martin Lockwood's* survey, and the results were of the most crucial importance not only to him, but to the whole future of research in this field. His theory of the Parasite Person (he had almost forgotten by now that the phrase was Ruth's originally, but of course he would give her due credit for this in the preface)— this theory of his needed to be supported by a mass of evidence substantial enough to hold its own against the Establishment opposition it was bound to encounter. And it *was* substantial enough, more and more of it was flowing in, day after day, from the answers to the amended questionnaire as administered by Ruth.

He picked up one of her latest interviews and glanced through it. And M 45 B, formerly a highly-successful business man, whose depression had been growing steadily worse over a number of months, and the business was beginning to suffer. By now it would have been on the rocks altogether, he claimed, if it hadn't been for his wife "turning up trumps" when the depression struck. Formerly a rather dim, ineffectual sort of woman, she had immediately summoned up reserves of energy such as he'd never dreamed she had in her.

"She's been marvellous—really marvellous! So cheerful, so patient, so full of courage! I don't know what I'd have done without her!"

You'd have got better, Mr. M 45 B, that's what you'd have done. Gleefully, Martin skimmed through the interview— which was a long one, and full of high significant quotes. Definitely, he would use it, perhaps among the case-histories.

And then he thought again about his recent doubts. Could Ruth really have made all this up? And *would* she? Whatever for? *She* wasn't getting anything out of the thesis, not even a decent wage. Not a wage at all, in fact; and as he recollected this Martin felt a surge of reassurance. For surely this fact nullified any possible motive for cheating? Why on earth would she be working for him at all, except (as she herself had claimed) from a genuine interest in the project, a genuine wish to discover the truth?

She *couldn't* have cheated, she just couldn't. Looking through the last batch of interviews, so detailed and so thorough, with verbatim replies so natural and convincing, Martin felt quite ashamed of himself for ever having doubted his capable and zealous assistant.

All the same, he must have a word with her about those two names in the Deaths Column. She mustn't be allowed to get away with it, even though she probably *wasn't* cheating in any important sense. He could guess exactly what had happened, because it had often enough happened to him in his interviewing days.

The way it went was this. You would get a marvellous and perfectly genuine interview off someone, by scrupulously honest means, and then, at the very end, when the whole thing was virtually in the bag, they'd turn around and refuse to give their name and address: sudden cold feet, perhaps, or they were illegal immigrants, or something. When this happened, what you were supposed to do was to scrap the whole interview: an absurd procedure, in Martin's view. Apart from the awful waste of labour involved, the practice could be held to be actually distorting the sample by introducing a bias against the type of people who like to remain anonymous. And so, a name and address on the form being a *sine qua non*, it was only common sense (or so it had always seemed to Martin) to provide one.

Yes, this was what must have happened to Ruth. Thrilled as she obviously was about how well the survey was going, and having in her hands two honestly-obtained interviews that so superbly vindicated the hypothesis, she just couldn't bear to scrap them for the sake of a mere formality like the obtaining of names and addresses. And so (just as he would have done in her place) she'd resorted to the time-honoured device of picking someone of appropriate age and sex out of the Death Column. . . .

But all so unnecessary! The silly girl! Did she really think he was the sort of boss who would tear strips off her for turning in an anonymous interview now and again. He must tell her that next time this happened, all she had to do was write "name and address withheld" at the top, and he would accept it unconditionally. As soon as she came in—which should be quite soon now, it was gone three—he'd raise the subject with her: quite amicably, of course, even laughing a bit, making it clear that he wasn't accusing her of cheating.

Softly, softly catchee monkey!

The monkey wasn't quite so easily caught.

"*What* Death Column? What do you mean?" she demanded; and when Martin explained—very gently, and smiling all the time to show her how lightly he took the whole matter —she proceeded, with one of those awful twists of feminine logic, to turn the tables on him, and put *him* on the defensive.

Who says? *Which* bloody paper? Well, go on, show me!— and of course he couldn't show her, because Helen had taken the paper back to school with her so as to return it to the colleague from whom she had purloined it.

"*Helen!*" She made the name sound like a new swear-word. "I might have known that it was Miss Bloody Nosey-Parker at the bottom of all this! She's been out to get me right from the start! Listen, Prof, I *will not* have this goddam whore of yours interfering with my work! I'll kill her if she does it again! Get it? Fuck her all you like, I don't care, but if she ever again gets her bloody claws on to any of my interviews, then I'm off! Finished! Vamoosed!—and you can do the rest of your effing interviews yourself. Right? There's at least forty of them still to do," she added spitefully, to frighten him; and it did; and she saw that it did. She lowered herself on to the couch, the short skirt riding up above her knees as usual, the thin mottled legs sticking out in front of her almost like weapons.

"Get it?" she repeated, eyes fixed on his face. "That bloody woman's not typing my interviews any more, is that understood? Not one more word of any of them. Ever again. Okay?"

Martin agreed at once, because he couldn't for the moment think of anything else to do. Then he began to consider what he had let himself in for.

"You mean *I'm* to type them? *Myself?*" he asked, horrified; and Ruth, sitting there like a small, newly-crowned empress on her throne, revelling in her sudden power to say "Off with his head" whenever she liked, nodded.

"Who else? *I* can't type. I told you, we had this careers mistress at school, and she was always saying, 'Whatever you do, girls, don't ever learn to type, else that's what you'll have to do.'"

That's what you have to do anyway, Martin could have told her, whether you've learnt or not: but this didn't seem to be quite the moment.

"Well . . . okay," he conceded reluctantly, and counting on it all blowing over before long, "But it's a bit rough, you know, at this stage. I've always relied on Helen to—"

"Of course you've relied on her! Of course you've leaned on her . . . told me how marvellous she is . . . the whole can't-do-without-her bit! Recognise it?—'Can't-do-without-her?' That's the victim talking about his Parasite Person . . . !

"And you know, Prof, it figures. Why do you think you've been so depressed ever since you moved in here? Why do you think leaving your wife didn't make you feel any better? It's because Beatrice wasn't your Parasite Person, she was merely beastly to you, and that's different. As soon as I'd talked to her for a bit I realised that she wasn't a Parasite Person, but merely a beastly person. Whereas Helen, bloody Saint Helen . . ."

Martin was irritated rather than upset by this tirade. Women were like that: once you get two of them into your life, on however innocent a basis, and sooner or later the jealous scenes start, and the tantrums. The thing to do was to keep your head down and make no promises.

"Okay, okay," he said, carefully not specifying what it was, precisely, that was, or was about to be, okay. "Calm down. No one's going to make you do anything you don't want."

Sensing that Ruth's anger, meeting no opposition, was already losing impetus, he decided that the moment was ripe to change the subject, and at the same time to re-establish his role as boss.

"That Timberley interview, Ruth. Did you do the call-back there, as I asked you to?"

It worked. At once she looked less like the Red Queen and more like a young research assistant—a *very* young one, indeed.

"Oh, Prof, I meant to tell you at once, the moment I got in, and I would have if you hadn't gone for me like that. It's great, it really is, the Timberley scene! It bears out everything we've been trying to prove, it's the case-history to end case-histories! The way it is, it's like this: old Mr. T. has had a heart attack—lugging that old lump around, I suppose—and has been whisked off to hospital. And the old lump?—what did I tell you? She was on her feet within hours of the ambulance fetching him away, and by the next day she was cleaning up the place, going to the shops, chatting with the neighbours. It was like magic, one of them said, to see her like that . . . see her changed into a normal ordinary woman after all those months.

"And I got a super interview out of her, Prof. The time you did her, it sounded like she never spoke at all but she speaks now all right—and how! She told me all about how her depression started, how it coincided with Mr. T.'s retirement, him being home all day kind of thing. She hates him, she says. She only realised she hated him when she saw him being driven away in the ambulance, and then it suddenly swept over her how terrified she'd been of him all these years. Such revelations! You've never heard anything like it—the archetypal Parasite Person he must have been! Just listen to this . . . !"

CHAPTER 22

Despite Martin's prudent policy of keeping his head down when jealous women were fighting over him, it still seemed to take the best part of a week before the thing began properly to subside.

In a way, it was more Helen's fault than Ruth's, Martin reluctantly decided, for though Ruth had blown her top (as she would have put it), had shouted and stormed and said horrible things about Helen, it wasn't as if Helen knew anything about it, and so it seemed a little unfair of her to be just as upset as if she had known.

Martin had gone about the whole business as kindly and tactfully as he knew how. He hadn't been such a fool as to tell Helen it was *Ruth's* idea that she should stop typing the interviews. He presented it, on the contrary, as his own idea, framed entirely with Helen's welfare in mind.

"It doesn't seem fair on you, darling, when you have such an awful lot to do anyway—running the flat, cooking marvellous meals for me, and a full-time job as well. It's not right."

A charming speech: but so much solicitude, so suddenly, naturally took Helen by surprise.

"But Martin, darling, I *love* doing your typing for you, you know I do! I've told you: I love the feeling of being involved in your work. And, you know, the exams are over now, there's only another week and a bit to the holidays . . . things are beginning to let up all round. I've got heaps of time now, truly I have."

So Martin had to start again.

"That's sweet of you darling. I do appreciate it, and don't

think I'm not grateful for all the marvellous amount of work you've done for me already. But you see, the thing is, darling . . ."

What on earth he was going to go on to say, Martin would never know: he had vaguely hoped that the sentence would finish itself somehow. But it never did. Helen was too quick for it.

"You mean *Ruth* doesn't like me typing her interviews! That's it, isn't it? She's asked you to stop me doing it . . ."

The speed of a woman's mind! More terrifying than any guided missile!

"Well . . ." Martin looked this way, looked that way, anywhere except at his beloved, and fumbled for words.

"Well, okay, Martin. If that's how you want it," and though she spoke quietly, he knew that she was bitterly hurt. "The only thing is, though, who *is* going to type them? They're coming in fast now, you know, you'll never have time to do them all yourself."

"Oh, Ruth will do them," Martin intervened eagerly, full of relief that the problem seemed to be changing from an emotional to a merely practical one. "She says she can do them herself, as she goes long. She says it will be easier that way. . . ."

"But I thought you told me she couldn't type?"

Helen seemed genuinely puzzled, and Martin found himself cursing, not for the first time, the concerned and loving attention that Helen paid to every single thing he told her. It left no loopholes anywhere.

In the end, of course, it all blew over. Helen wasn't one to bear grudges, and soon she had settled into her new no-typing routine quite happily. Really, there was plenty for her to do, what with running the flat and protecting him from visitors, telephone calls, or anything else tiresome that might disrupt the flow of his creativity.

It was going marvellously well, really marvellous. "*Interesting*," his supervisor had cautiously pronounced, pulling at his moustache uneasily and trying to hide (lest the cat should jump the wrong way) that he was really quite impressed.

By this time, however, Martin was less bothered by his supervisor's opinion than he could ever had imagined possible: because by this time all sorts of other things were beginning to happen. He had written, at top speed, and in a state bordering on panic lest someone else should get in ahead of him with the same idea, a short summary of his findings for one of the learned journals, and it had been accepted almost at once, with a nice letter from the Editor thrown in, predicting that his readers would find Martin's ideas "stimulating and provocative."

And this was not all. Somehow, the Press had got on to it, and two reporters, one of them on a national paper, had rung him up and asked for an interview. In the event, neither of them had actually turned up, despite Martin's alacrity in accepting: but no doubt the Press were like that, he hadn't had any dealings with them before; and anyway, it was still very exciting. Even to be stood-up by a top-ranking journalist is quite an experience for one whose whole life has been lived so far in tantalising obscurity.

The local paper had done him proud.

"Is there a Parasite Person in your Midst?" had been the headline, and a not-too-inaccurate summary of his theory had followed, together with a very flattering picture of him sitting at his desk, finger-tips together, and with an enigmatic smile on his lips. It wasn't often that photographs came out just right like this, both flattering and exactly like you. Martin sat and looked at it for hours.

At least, he would have done, if the pressures hadn't been building up the way they were. As he had predicted at the beginning, the concept of a Parasite Person draining away your talents and energies, gorging itself on your remarkable gifts and undoubted genius, touched a chord in all kinds of people. There was something in it for everybody, and there, at the top of the pile, turning out corroborative evidence like a factory turning out tins of cat-food, sat Martin Lockwood.

Keeping up the pace: that was the problem now. The heady joys of success—the euphoria, the incredulous joy—were all that he had ever dreamed. What he hadn't quite envisaged was the way you had to keep at it to fulfil the ever-mounting, ever-flattering demands to which, in his jubilation, he kept saying "yes" . . . and "yes" . . . and again "yes." Already he was committed to an article on "Parapsychology and the Parasite Person"; and another, for a business magazine, on "Parasite Persons in Management." Most urgent of all, there was a piece for *Readers' Roundabout* on "The Parasite Person in Myth and Legend." They were actually going to pay him for it, and in his headlong delight he'd said that he could produce it by the weekend.

Myths. There must be hundreds of myths illustrating his theme . . . thousands of them. Why spend hours—days—weeks—poring over those weighty historical tomes that filled shelf after shelf after shelf of the Humanities Wing of the library? One myth is as good as another. Anyone can make up a myth. Slipping a new sheet into the typewriter, he found his fingers almost doing it for him:

"There is a story"—(well, there is now)—"of two bullocks who broke loose from the abattoir and went careering round the town, to the terror of the populace. No one dared try and catch them, everyone rushed inside and bolted and barred their doors.

Within half an hour, both bullocks were back at the abattoir, lowing to be allowed in . . ."

Where will I say this story come from? Hell, why should I say anything? A story like that wouldn't be copyright, even if it was genuine. If they lean on me about it, I'll say Venezuela. Who wants to go to Venezuela? It's delectable places, like Yugoslavia, that you have to be careful about, where proving you wrong can be combined with a delightful holiday, sea-bathing and scuba-diving and the rest.

Of course, for the thesis itself he'd have to provide refer-ences, footnotes about sources, and so forth. *Readers' Rounda-bout* might not be too bothered, but the learned journals would, and if the name of Martin Lockwood was to be honoured in *both* fields, in the Groves of Academe as well as in the bestseller lists, then he must watch his references.

References . . . references . . . Were they really such a stumbling-block? Even on the learned journals, do the editor and his staff *really* check on every last one of your references? Especially if these references happen to come from a fairly out-of-date number of a small and now-defunct journal . . . ?

Next afternoon—and it was an afternoon well-spent—Mar-tin was once again to be found in the Humanities Section of the library making a list of the journals which had folded up within the last ten years or so.

There seemed to be dozens of them! Delightedly, he copied out the titles; and then turned his attention to authors. What sort of names did the authors of obscure psychological articles tend to have? Looking through the still-extant journals he found—again to his delight—that an incredible number of the names in this field were not only foreign, but virtually unpro-nounceable and unspellable as well—Odajnyk, Wicsniowiecki, and such. Who would have the nerve to bandy names like *that* with him at his Viva, or across an editorial desk . . . ?

He almost crowed aloud in his quiet alcove among the li-brary shelves. Anyone could invent names like that, and he defied anyone—anyone at all, no matter how expert—to prove that such a character *didn't* exist, and that it *hadn't*, some time in the sixties, written such-and-such an article for such-and-such a now defunct journal?

He'd guessed it would be easy, but even he hadn't guessed it would be *this* easy. That evening, the quotes flowed from his fingers as if in a dream, and it was fun, real up-roaring fun, matching the right unpronounceable name to the right type of quote. So engrossed was he in this fascinating task that when the phone went, and Helen answered it (as of course she almost always did, these days), he was barely aware of it. But after a while, something in her voice caught his attention, and he found himself listening.

"Yes, that's right," she was saying: and then, "Oh, about six or seven weeks ago, I should think. . . . Yes, he came to interview them. Yes. . . . yes . . ."

And then came a pause, quite a long one. Then:

"Oh dear! Oh, I *am* sorry! Yes. . . . Yes, I suppose so, it *is* a mercy in a way, she'd have been so absolutely lost without him. . . ."

Then, after another long pause, and in a slightly different tone:

"Oh! Oh . . . well. . . . Just a moment. . . ."

Here Helen turned from the phone.

"Sorry to interrupt you, darling," she said, "but it's about the Timberleys. . . . Some rather sad news. Mr. Timberley had a heart attack, and—"

Martin was impatient. He'd already heard all about it.

"Yes, yes," he interrupted. "Ruth told me. She says that Mrs. T. . . ."

"Only survived him by a few hours," finished Helen. "Of course, in a way, it was a mercy, because—"

She'd got it all wrong, muddled it somehow, or else this woman she was talking to had; but what the hell? He was itching to get back to his work.

"And so . . . ?" he inquired, in that tone which shuts people up with minimum delay.

"And so," Helen repeated, in the dry tone she sometimes used when she thought he was being a bit heartless. "And so Mrs. Hobbs—the neighbour—she wants to know what to do about the budgerigar? There doesn't seem to be any family, you see, and she's ringing us because your card, Martin, was the only clue she had to *anybody* who might have known them. But the thing is—the immediate thing—this budgerigar.

She can't take it herself, she says, because she has two cats, and so just *wonders*—if you don't mind, that is—if *we'd* take it for the time being? I could fetch it after school tomorrow, it would be no trouble. It would be nice, don't you think, to feel that there's *something* we can do for the poor souls . . . ?"

Martin couldn't see that it would be nice at all. And he didn't believe Helen when she said that the bird would be no trouble. Pets were *always* a trouble, and it was just silly to pretend otherwise.

"His name is Tweetie," Helen pleaded, just as if this made any difference to the problem; but when he looked up to protest, and met her eager, anxious gaze, he changed his mind. After all that fuss about Ruth and the typing, only so recently resolved, he didn't want *another* fuss, this time about a budgerigar, for God's sake.

"I'll clean the cage myself—and feed him—and everything," Helen was pleading; and on this understanding, Martin permitted himself a grudging nod of acquiescence.

And the next time the telephone went, it was as if God himself was ringing up to reward Martin's generosity and forebearance.

It was Television. They wanted to do a programme about the Parasite Person, with him, Martin Lockwood, for the centre-piece.

It had happened! This was the moment towards which his whole life had been leading. He had arrived!

CHAPTER 23

Ruth, when she arrived on Monday morning, wasn't quite as thrilled by the news as he'd expected her to be. In fact, she sulked a bit, just at first.

"*I* want to be on it," she said, "It's not *fair!* It was *my* idea. I'*m* the one who's done practically all the work!"

She sounded so like a small child done out of a treat that Martin could not help smiling.

"But *of course*, Ruth! You've been a most wonderful help to me, and *of course* I'm going to give you credit for it, all the credit in the world! You're going to be in my preface, practically in letters of gold! You'll be the star! But this television thing—you must see, Ruth—dear this is a bit different. I have no control over it, you see; who they put in the programme and who they don't. It's a terrific thing for me that they've asked me at all: I can't—not at this stage—start asking favours, now can I? Not this first time," he hastened to add, seeing her expression. "But another time . . . later on . . . when I'm in a position to pull strings, perhaps. . . ."

The vagueness of these promises was all too evident. He laid his hand on her shoulder.

"Now, come on, Ruth! Snap out of it! The more of a success I am this time, the sooner I'll be a man of influence, able to swing things for you! So come on, let's get going. I want to get this stuff in some sort of order. I have to be ready, you see, for anything they may be going to ask me. . . . I want to know exactly where we're at. . . ."

Whether it was his adoption of one of her own favourite

slang expressions, or whether it was the general tenor of his conciliatory little speech, Martin could not tell, but anyway, she brightened up, and quite quickly became her usual enthusiastic self.

"Dreams. . . . You must try and get them to ask you about dreams, Prof, because we've got some jolly good ones. . . . Remember that one about the rats . . . ? That woman who kept on about how supportive and wonderful her husband was being, and then, every night, she had this dream about rats being in the bed with her, gnawing at her flesh? Here—here we are—F 55 C. . . ." All the while she'd been speaking, Ruth's deft fingers had been sorting through the piles of interviews—quite a few of them still awaiting typing. As he'd predicted, without Helen the typing was getting sadly in arrears. Still, they were fairly legible, and Ruth quickly found what she was looking for: some more dreams of this nature. Not quite so super as the rat one, perhaps, but of similar import. She gathered them into a small pile, separate from the rest.

"Good idea," said Martin, watching her approvingly. "We'll sort them into categories according to highlights, regardless of age and sex . . . and mark with a star, Ruth, the really good quotes. Here—have a look at this one! The accountant chappie —remember?—who was hell-bent on convincing you that his mother actually *enjoyed* being depressed! Listen—how about this for a quote?—

" 'It's my opinion that people in general *want* to be miserable. They seek for unhappiness as for a crock of gold which, once found, will absolve them from all further effort. Unhappiness is Life's big, cushiony armchair—once you sit down in it, and no one will ever be able to get you to exert yourself again. It's the place below which you can't fall, it's the possession you never need fear losing . . .'

"See if you can find some others, Ruth, on these lines. This is something I'll need to go into in a big way—the Parasite Person trying to convince himself that he's doing his victim a favour . . . trying to assuage his guilt feelings while continuing his meal. . . ."

Between them, they found several to illustrate this theme: and then they moved on to examples—and there were many— of the victims themselves feeling abject gratitude towards their persecutors: the "I don't-know-what-I'd-do-without-him" Brigade, as Ruth labelled them.

It was fascinating. The two of them worked together like professional tennis players, in perfect rapport, backing each other up, anticipating each other's every move.

Once again, Martin had that feeling of something almost supernatural being at work. Everything he tried to make fit, *did* fit . . . it wasn't just those sub-atomic physicists and their particles after all; it was the Martin Lockwood Project too, the whole universe was going along with it, he was swimming with the tide of things. How else could the facts—quotes—everything—be falling into place like this, exactly as he wanted them? It was as if they came running at his command, gathering round like well-trained dogs at the sound of the master's whistle. His mind seemed to have grown an extra dimension, it felt choked with light.

Some of the material, he knew, was still very hypothetical, and yet he did not feel that by presenting it as established fact he was giving way to temptation: rather that by following his instincts in preference to cold reason he had come out on the royal road to truth, with every step he took bringing him nearer and nearer to the goal.

When at last they paused for a bread-and-cheese lunch, Martin poured them each a stiff drink.

"We deserve it!" he said, and they raised glasses.

"To your bestseller, with my name on it in gold letters!" cried Ruth, and added:

"What d'you bet, Prof, that within a year Action Man will have been ousted from all the toy-shops, and been replaced by Parasite Person?

"And the Gift Departments will be piled high with Parasite Mugs, and Parasite Place-Mats . . . !"

They laughed exultantly, they clinked glasses: and now, joining exuberantly in the celebration, there came a shrill voice from the kitchen:

"Pretty Tweetie!" it yelled, "Pretty Tweetie, Pretty Tweetie!"

Tweetie was loving his new life, full of clear sounds, bright daylight, and life surging all around him. He'd never known anything like it:

"Pretty Tweetie! Pretty Tweetie! Pretty Tweetie!"

"What's that?" said Ruth sharply, setting her glass down almost with a bang, so that it slopped over a bit on to the polished table. For some reason, it never occurred to Martin to tell a lie.

"Oh, that's the Timberley budgie," he said carelessly. "Helen brought it over."

"*Helen* brought it? Why did she do that?" and now Martin did begin to sense that he had put a foot wrong.

"Well, because . . ."

He stopped, not so much from nervousness—though by now he was indeed nervous—as because he truly couldn't remember. Some terribly boring reason it had been, concerning a neighbour and somebody's two cats: not at all the sort of thing he was in the habit of listening to, let alone remembering. By now, the only thing he could recall about the wretched bird was that he'd been agin-it, and that Helen had coaxed him into acquiescing.

"Well . . ." he began again, still wondering how he was going to go on: but luckily Ruth didn't press her question. Quietly, she walked out into the kitchen, and stood staring at the creature for long minutes, her eyes so wide, so dark, that Martin wondered momentarily if she suffered from bird-phobia. There was such a thing, he knew, but somehow Ruth didn't seem the sort of person who'd suffer from it.

And nor she was. Hardly had the possibility crossed his mind than she gave a short laugh.

"How very peculiar of her!" she commented. "Whatever did she want it for?"

Martin missed the veiled threat in the question.

"Oh, well, there was no one to look after it, you see," he explained easily. "With the Timberleys both being dead, she thought . . ."

"*Dead?*"

Even before Ruth's interjection, Martin had realised his mistake; but it was too late.

"So *that's* what she told you, was it?" Ruth exploded. "That they were both dead? She's been spying on me, hasn't she, that whore of yours? She's been checking-up on my interviews! And *you've* been putting her up to it, you must have done!"

"I have not!" Martin's outrage was genuine: never would he have employed Helen in such a role. "I wouldn't dream of it! When have I ever checked on any of your interviews? As a matter of fact, I thought your Timberley interview was superb —I told you so at the time. It never crossed my mind to question it, you know that very well. As to Helen—she got the wrong end of the stick, that's all . . . listening to idle gossip . . . a garbled story from some garrulous neighbour. . . . She's not trained for this kind of work the way you and I are. . . ."

Noting that Ruth seemed slightly mollified by the implied compliment, Martin set himself to follow up this small success by further blandishments. He assured her, over and over again, that his confidence in her integrity was absolute; and he attempted, too, to convince her that Helen's visit to the Timberleys had been entirely innocent, a simple errand of mercy born of a misconception.

"She didn't even know you'd *done* any interviewing there," he affirmed, hoping against hope that this was true—since the interview in question had been lying about on his desk for days, there could be no certainty about it—"so do please stop worrying about it, my dear."

Whether Ruth had indeed stopped worrying about it was hard to tell, but at least she stopped talking about it: a big improvement from Martin's point of view, and one which enabled them to get back to work, and to spend the rest of the afternoon in a reasonably profitable manner.

After Ruth had gone, Martin still worked on, through the evening and far into the night. The glory of inspiration was still upon him, and when all possible preparations for the TV interview were completed, he threw himself into finishing Chapter I of his bestseller. This, together with the now completed synopsis, was to go this week to the lucky, lucky publisher he'd selected from the *Writers' and Artists' Yearbook*. It was a somewhat different synopsis from the one he'd submitted to his supervisor, but what the hell? He no longer cared a damn what his supervisor thought or didn't think, for Fame was already within his grasp, thesis or no thesis. He was on his way.

CHAPTER 24

After the unfortunate contretemps about the Timberleys, Martin had been afraid that Ruth would turn up in a bad mood the next morning, and that he would have to devote valuable time to bringing her round. So he was greatly relieved when she walked in looking quite her old self.

"I've come to blackmail you," she said. "I want £55,000."

Martin stared. She was joking, of course.

"Otherwise," she continued, settling herself comfortably in her usual corner of the settee, "otherwise, I'll tell them. The whole bloody bunch of them. Your supervisor—your publisher—all those editors—I'll tell them that the whole thing's a fraud. That you've cooked your evidence . . . that your interviews are all fakes. . . ."

Too dazed to take in the full implications of what she was saying, Martin pounced on the one thing which could be clearly challenged.

"Fakes? What do you mean, they're all fakes? Hell, you did them yourself, nearly all of them . . . !"

"Yes. That's how I know," she explained, pleased with her own logic. "I made them all up, you see, every single last one of them. That's why I can say with such absolute authority that they *are* fakes. . . ."

"But . . . Hell . . . !" Martin reeled, struggling for words. "In that case, it's *yourself* you're condemning . . . !"

"Not so, Prof, and you know it! It's *your* job to see that your assistants don't cheat, not theirs! You should have checked up on me. You should have done call-backs. You know quite well you should; then none of this could have happened."

The self-righteous note in her voice as she administered this reproof was insufferable. Martin stood speechless, dumb with shock, unable to collect his wits. She was joking. She must be joking.

"All those faked sources, too," she continued, in the same quite pleasant tone. "You think I didn't know? You think a poor dumb drop-out like me wouldn't be able to figure it out? Believe me, Prof, I've done enough grubbing in libraries to know that you *couldn't* have tracked down that much in a single afternoon—and from a dozen different disciplines, too! It would take half a year. Even a dumb second-year drop-out knows the score to *that* extent.

"Besides, I went along and checked out a few of them. *Funny*, I thought, so many articles from defunct, out-of-print journals? And that's what your supervisor's going to think, too, when I call his attention to it. *Funny*, he's going to think . . ."

"My supervisor . . ." Martin stopped. His heart was racing but he managed to keep his voice calm, even authoritative. "If I were you, Ruth, I'd keep him out of this. There's such a thing as trust, you know—or maybe you don't, but there is. Trust between colleagues. He wouldn't listen to you. He'd never dream of checking on every tiny detail of my work just on your say-so! A man in my position, too! It would be . . . well . . . undignified . . . !"

"And how! That's been my thinking, too!

"But look, Prof, it doesn't *have* to happen. None of it has to. Once I've got my £55,000, I'll not only keep quiet about the swindle, but I'll positively back you up in any further lies you like to tell. And that's a promise. I'm a good liar, as you must have noticed. A top-ranking, experienced, bare-faced liar, and a sweet, innocent young girl with it; they'll never suspect *me*. We can't lose.

"So come on, Prof, the money, please."

She reached out her brown little hand, with its childishly

bitten nails, pulled open the third drawer down of his desk, and handed him his cheque book.

Joke or not, this was too much. How the hell did she know which drawer to look in, anyway?

"Leave my things alone!" he commanded. "Shut that drawer at once!"

She obeyed instantly; and a little reassured by this—it gave him the feeling of having regained the upper hand—he continued:

"What the hell makes you think I've *got* £55,000? What sort of salary do you imagine we poor bloody lecturers . . . ?"

"I don't know and I don't care what salary you get, you can starve on it for all I care. No, it's your house I'm talking about. Your half-share of the 'Marital Home'—I saw the letters from the legal-freaks in your ex-wife's desk; I had a quick decco while she was yapping on the phone one time. £110,000 it's been valued at, and you're getting half, right? £55,000 that comes to. She can do sums, too, this dumb little drop-out, she can actually divide by two, would you credit it?"

Here, once again, was something that he could contradict.

"I'm afraid, my poor child, that you've got it all wrong," he said. "That's what comes of poking and prying around in other people's desks, you just come up with the wrong end of the stick. Let me give you a bit of reality on the thing. Those were just the preliminary letters that you found. Since then, we've decided—Beatrice and I—that it would be much simpler for her to keep the whole house in exchange for not getting any alimony. *She* doesn't want to move, you see, and *I* don't want to pay out good money to support her for the rest of her life, so it seems a good idea all round. She thinks she can make a living by taking in lodgers—*lodgers*, my God, she couldn't even run the place decently for just the two of us, never mind lodgers—still, that's her worry. And theirs too, of course, poor devils, but anyway not mine. . . ."

He paused. Why was he confiding his private business to this treacherous little bitch who sat watching him with bright, bird-like eyes, head on one side, waiting for a chance to score off him.

He was *not* going to be intimidated. It was ridiculous. She couldn't really have imagined she was going to get away with it.

"So you see, I haven't *got* £55,000," he concluded carefully, watching for her reaction.

"That so? Well, that's your bad luck, isn't it, Prof? It's a shame, but this settles it. I'll have to tell them. Has your publisher got the manuscript yet?—Oh, a pity, I was going to start with him, but it would be nice for him to read it first, wouldn't it? So okay, I'll start with *Psychology for Everyone*, and the rubbish you wrote for them about 'Parasite Parenting.' That'll have gone to press already, it'll make them a laughing-stock, they'll be charmed, won't they? And then that Para-psychology Whatsit, who were so thrilled with your piece—I wonder how thrilled they'll be *now*? You know how hypersensitive they are to fraud in that racket, they need to be. . . .

"I think I'll leave your supervisor till last: *his* face when he hears it I want to relax and enjoy. . . ."

So she *did* mean it. She really did. Martin's heart was thumping so that it nearly hurt; he felt the sweat breaking out on his forehead. He had to fight to keep control.

"You realise that this is blackmail?" he said coldly. "And that blackmail is a criminal offence, almost equivalent to murder? You could get twelve or fourteen years in prison. . . ."

She laughed, really amused.

"What, *me*? You must be joking, Prof! I'm only a kid you know, hardly more than a child. Nothing I do is *my* fault, it's my Mother's fault . . . or my Dad's fault . . . or Society's fault! *Someone's* bloody fault, anyway, not mine. They shouldn't have brought me up like that, should they? It *seemed* okay at the time. It felt like a real good scene, but it couldn't have been, could it, or I wouldn't have turned out like this.

"So you see, Prof, I've got nothing to lose and everything to gain. I can push you to the limit—in fact, I could be real mean, and go *on* pushing you, whenever I felt like it. But I won't do that, I'll be content with a lump sum down here and now, and that'll be the finish. Fifty-five thou, and we call it a day, right?"

"I tell you I haven't got—"

"Oh, that's what they all say! I've blackmailed people before, you know, Prof, and it's my experience they always find the money somehow. Especially smug, swollen-headed middle-aged failures who can't admit that they're failures. *Or* that they're middle-aged. . . ."

"You must have struck lucky, then," he retorted bitterly. "Not all 'middle-aged failures' are like that. This one isn't, for a start. This one is going straight to the police."

She laughed again, delightedly.

"And tell them what? I can deny everything, you know. I can say I never worked for you at all—never did any interviews or anything. There's no one to say I did. Since I never got paid anything, your Grants people will never have heard of me, and they'll back me up when I say I've never had anything to do with it.

"Sorry, Prof, but I've got you over a barrel. You can't prove a thing."

It was ridiculous. There *must* be a way out.

"Okay, so the Grants people don't know you've been involved in the survey: but lots of people *do*. Helen, for example. Right from the beginning she's been . . ."

"If Helen interferes, I'll kill her! I've had enough of that bitch's interference, I told you! This is between you and me, Prof. No one else, okay?"

"You can say that, but you know, Ruth, it just won't wash. All right, so we leave Helen out of it—and God knows the last thing I want is to have her dragged into such a sordid mess— but there's a lot of other people who must know by now that we've been working together. Neighbours. The people downstairs. For weeks they've seen you coming in and out of the flat at all hours . . ."

"—At all the hours when your live-in girlfriend is safely out at her job! Be your age, Prof! Do you really imagine that they're telling each other we've been *working?* Or that they'll tell the police anything of the kind either? Really, Prof, you want your head examined!"

Martin was cornered, and knew it. He could see only one—very despicable—avenue of escape.

"Walter," he muttered, almost choking on the loathed name, "Walter knows that . . ."

"Oh, *Walter!* Don't worry about Walter, Prof, he'll say whatever I ask him to say. He can tell them, for a start, that you never checked up on his interviews, either. Very obliging, Walter is, very imperturbable. With that big fat smile of his he'd make a perfect Parasite Person, if only there were such things. Pity! Leave Walter to me, Prof, he's not looking for trouble. Besides, he likes me. You wouldn't think anyone could, would you?"

Martin cursed himself for ever having brought the wretched lad's name into the discussion at all, especially in the role of potential saviour. The humiliation was awful. He'd never hit a woman before, had somehow never felt the need of it, but in this moment he could have smashed his fist into that blandly smiling little face and felt nothing but joy.

Rage, though, would get him nowhere, except perhaps into the police court. Nor, any longer, had he any authority left to wield. All that was left to him now was to plead with her. Humiliation could go on further.

"Look, Ruth," he began, forcing himself to speak placatingly, reasonably. "Look, we've worked so well together so far . . . surely we aren't going to let it end like this? We're on the same wavelength, somehow . . . there's been such rapport between us . . . surely you must have felt it . . . ?"

"Of course I've felt it! You know what it consists of, though, don't you? You know why it is we work so well together? It's

because we share the criminal mentality. Neither of us has a
conscience of any kind at all. I can intimidate my loving par-
ents by bogus suicide attempts into giving me a nice big allow-
ance so I don't have to work: you can perpetrate a bare-faced
fraud on colleagues who trust you. Neither of us cares a damn
about anyone in the whole world except ourselves, and that's
what has kept us together. The gangsters' moll in me cries out
to the gangster in you and gets answered every time, haven't
you noticed?

"That's what we have between us, Prof; and if you give me
that £55,000 we can go on having it. We could really go
places, you and I. Both of us heartless, unscrupulous, totally
without principles: the sort of people who will stop at nothing,
who don't hesitate to blackmail our dearest friends . . ."

She paused, watching this sink in.

"Well, how about it, Prof? If you don't want to play, then
just say so, and I'll ring up all these people and expose you for
the fraud you are. It'll be fun—especially those television guys
you've been getting so excited about. That's going to be the
biggest fun of all. It's a bit of luck, isn't it, that you never
asked them to put *me* in the programme, like I wanted you to?
If you had, I couldn't have done any of this. Could I?"

The little monkey! So *this* was what the whole thing had
been about! Not genuine blackmail at all, but just a mischie-
vous trick to scare him half to death as a punishment for not
getting her on to the programme!

He could have laughed aloud in his relief. The cheek of it!
And she *had* scared him half to death, he had to hand it to
her. Hell, he might have had a heart-attack, it had actually felt
like that at one point.

Still, he couldn't bring himself to scold her. He felt (as is
not uncommon among victims) such a rush of gratitude for
the cessation of his torments, that he quite forgot to feel any
resentment towards his tormentor.

"You little *monkey!*" he said aloud. "You really quite took
me in for a minute or two, and I don't mind admitting it. I re-

ally thought you were serious! Look, I'm sorry, my dear, about the programme. For myself, I'd love to have you on it, you know that. Next time they ring me up, I'll have a word with them about you. I promise you I'll do what I can."

What he could do was absolutely nil, of course: but, as everyone knows, it's the thought that counts.

CHAPTER 25

He'd always known he would love being on television. It had been his secret dream for as long as he could remember, and now the dream was about to be fulfilled.

He'd arrived at the studios ridiculously early, so nervous had he been lest he should arrive late, and had sat in the entrance hall for more than an hour watching the celebrities making their way in and out, and hugging to himself the thought that now, at last, he was one of them. Or nearly. Or would be, anyway, before the evening was over.

Of course, they might not *all* be celebrities, these vaguely impressive passers-by. Some of them might be electricians and messengers and things. But somehow it made little difference. Here they all were, anyway, at the glittering hub of things, and he, Martin Lockwood, was among them.

This was the place where he belonged: had always belonged. He was coming into his heritage.

They were all charming to him. With bright, welcoming smiles they looked him up on their lists, showed him where to wait, brought him coffee in a plastic beaker. Well, he hadn't expected it to be a golden goblet, had he? And indeed it had no need to be, for it was like the nectar of the gods anyway. This was *Television*, was it not, and this was himself, Martin Lockwood, taking his place among the mighty. It would take more than a plastic cup of warmed-up coffee with blobs of powdered milk floating in it to destroy the glory of it all.

The make-up room was wonderful, too. He'd been startled, at first, by the notion that a bronzed upstanding he-man like himself should require such adornment; but the make-up girl, like everyone else, had been charming.

"That's what they all say," she assured him. "But you'll be surprised how natural it looks on camera. Your friends will all tell you—and you'll be able to see for yourself, I daresay, if they do a repeat of you. I expect they will."

She laughed a little, amiably, as she proceeded deftly with her task, and Martin felt his heart swelling with a mixture of nervousness and pride. "I expect they will," she'd said—was she just being polite, or did she actually know something? It couldn't be her business, exactly, but no doubt there was a busy grapevine here just like everywhere else, and he had, after all, been introduced to her by name.

His face, in the mirror, seemed to glow with a new confidence, a new assurance that had nothing to do with the make-up. Already, he looked like a celebrity, and he wondered if the girl had noticed?

Never mind. She would next time. "You mean *the* Martin Lockwood?" she would say with bated breath next time they were introduced.

The studio was so full of lights and wires and hurrying young men that at first Martin found it quite difficult to orientate himself. He was introduced to his fellow-members on the panel —the two of them who had already arrived, that is. One was a professor of psychology from some Northern university, the other a stout white-haired lady in a scarlet trouser-suit who had written a book about something or other, he couldn't gather what, but it didn't matter, he smiled enthusiastically and said. "How interesting!" and then the three of them chatted, rather stiltedly, "getting to know one another" until the fourth member of the panel arrived and was ushered into their midst.

At first, he didn't recognise her. In a slinky, silvery evening dress and with her greasy elf-locks done up in the glittering coils on top of her head, Ruth Ledbetter looked like a total stranger, and a most distinguished one at that. By the time he took in who she was, she was already in her seat, two places away from him, and chatting easily with her neighbour, the Northern professor, as if this sort of thing was all in the day's work to her.

The little devil! He couldn't help admiring it. How on earth had she wangled herself on to the programme? Cheek, of course, sheer, brazen cheek—it could get you anywhere, especially if you were a beautiful young girl. He'd never thought of Ruth Ledbetter as beautiful before—rather the reverse—but tonight, in this get-up, perfectly groomed, and with that unwonted air of aristocratic elegance—beautiful was the only word. Her eyes, which he'd never really noticed before, were green as a cat's under the arc lights.

The interviewer, a good-looking young man who could not be more than thirty, was as charming as everyone else had been, if possible more so. The programme started with him talking to Martin easily, and with genuine interest, about the nature of this fascinating new project; drawing him out, encouraging him, and asking exactly the questions that he had hoped to be asked. Under this expert and sympathetic guidance, Martin found himself answering fluently, easily. All his nervousness had gone, now that the programme had actually begun, and he suddenly realised, with a little leap of the heart, that he was a "natural" for this kind of thing. Secretly, he had always known he would be, but how wonderful to have it confirmed, in front of all the world! All his friends would be watching, all his colleagues, all those people who'd got ahead of him in the academic rat-race—*this* would show them! *This* would make them sit up and take notice of him at last! These moments of absolute triumph, of total unqualified success, were moments of such happiness as he had never known.

It couldn't go on for ever, obviously. Other members of the panel had to be given their turn. Smiling and suave as ever, the interviewer turned to Ruth.

"And now, Miss Ledbetter, I wonder if you could tell us a little bit about *your* share in this exciting enterprise? I understand that you've been working as Mr. Lockwood's assistant for some time now—collecting information for him, and generally helping with the great work?"

There was a tiny pause. Ruth had been looking down into her lap as he addressed her. Now she raised her head and looked her questioner full in the face.

"No, I haven't collected any information for him," she replied, "There's been no need. He makes it all up, you see. Every single interview—all the case-histories, everything— they're all completely phoney. He's made the whole lot up to fit this crazy hypothesis of his. The whole thing is a swindle from beginning to end, a complete and utter con. . . ."

What happened next, how they set about cutting-off the programme, Martin would never know. The moment was so appalling, so shocking, so totally unendurable, that he blacked out on it completely. He retained only a sharp little cameo-portrait of that pleasant smiling face grown icy with shock . . . of a stunned silence . . . and then of a cold voice saying, "I'm afraid, Mr. Lockwood, this goes beyond apologies. . . . This is a kind of let-down we've never experienced before. . . .

After that came the endless corridors . . . walking, walking, as if in a nightmare . . . and now, somehow, here he was in this taxi, with the street lights flicking past like all the years of his life, and somehow, beside him in the vehicle, Ruth too was seated.

She was saying something. What it was he neither heard nor cared. For all he knew, she might be saying she was sorry.

"Shut up!" he hissed. "I don't want to hear a word from you ever again. I just want to get home to Helen."

Helen. Somehow, Helen would find a way of diminishing the agony. She would have heard of someone else that this sort of thing had happened to, making him feel that he was not utterly alone in his disgrace. No, she would say, of course he hadn't ruined his whole life! No life is ruined by one single disaster—in fact a disaster can sometimes be a springboard into something new and wonderful, in some totally unexpected way.

Everyone makes mistakes, she would say, even frightful mistakes, but a brave man can go forward and live them down. And Martin *was* a brave man, she would assure him; and hearing the words spoken in her loving voice, he would be able to believe them.

A laughing-stock among his colleagues for the rest of his life? —Listen, Darling, do you remember that famous actress we heard on the radio, who was asked what was the most important thing she'd learned in all her long career? And do you remember her answer: *"Everybody* forgets *everything!"*

His scientific reputation in ruins? Not necessarily, she would say, her grey eyes earnest and thoughtful. Sometimes it can be the false hypotheses just as much as the true ones which help science on its way. Look at Semelweiss, propounding the theory that it was the devils rising from the corpses which were causing puerperal fever in the maternity ward adjoining the mortuary. The hypothesis had been absolutely wrong, of course, quite ridiculous really, and yet it had paved the way to the bacterial theory of infections, and all the fantastic medical advances which have followed . . .

Yes, these were the sort of things Helen would say. In a few minutes she would be saying them, making them real for him in her sweet voice, with her arms around him, her love and loyalty unshaken.

"Helen? But she won't be there." Ruth sounded slightly surprised. "I've killed her, you see."

She waited a moment, and when Martin did not answer, she went on, slightly aggrieved:

"I told you I would. I told you I'd kill her if she interfered again—and she *did* interfere. She'd found my Timberley interview you see, and she stood there saying it was all lies, and wouldn't give it back to me. I wanted my other interviews too, the ones in my own handwriting that might be recognised, but she just stood there, blocking my way, and tried to stop me getting at your desk.

"I warned her. I warned her twice. 'Let me get at that desk!' I said. I told her I'd got a knife: and I had. I told her that if she didn't get out of my way I'd kill her: and I did.

"That was fair, wasn't it? She'd been warned."

In the wavering light of the taxi she turned towards Martin as if for assent to this proposition: and when he neither moved nor spoke, she went on:

"All right, *be* like that! But don't start imagining you'll get anywhere by setting the police on me, because you won't. Like I told you, I'm only a kid, and when they hear how I've been seduced and then heartlessly abandoned by a man more than twice my age. . . . And don't waste breath pointing out that you *didn't* seduce me, because who's going to believe it? *I* shall stick to it that you did, and what with me being an inexperienced young girl and you being a hardened lecher who within a few weeks has betrayed three women in quick succession, starting with your wife. . . . Well, what do you *expect* everyone to think? Can you wonder that my innocent little heart is broken? That I'm beside myself with uncontrollable jealousy?

"A *crime passionnel*, that's what it'll be, Prof: and what with me being so touchingly young, hardly more than a child, I'll bet you anything I don't get a prison sentence at all: just the Welfare and all that jazz; and believe me, I know how to make rings round *them* all right.

"Honestly, Prof, teenage is a wonderful age to be! Maybe you remember? You are at the very peak of your powers, mental and physical, and yet nothing you do is your fault! It's the archetypal eat-your-cake-and-have-it bonanza of all time, and am I making the most of it while I can! Suicide—fraud—blackmail—and now murder! I shall get away with the lot of it—just you watch!"

In the dark interior of the taxi she fairly bounced about on the seat with glee, and the swiftly-passing lights flickered across her pointed face like goblin fire.

Presently, they were outside the flat. The taxi had come to a halt, and money—presumably Martin's, though he had no recollection of having taken out his wallet—had been passed through the window to the driver. Already the vehicle was on its way again, apparently with the murderess still inside, for now he found himself standing alone on the dark wet pavement outside the house. His keys, by some automatic process of which he could recollect nothing, were already in his hand.

The front door closed behind him, and step by step, in heavy darkness, and with awful slowness, his feet mounted the stairs towards the flat.

Helen is dead. The words came slowly, one-two-three, in time with his footfalls, and they meant nothing.

Up he went, up and up, in the darkness and the silence, and the words went with him, round and round the bends of the staircase, and still they meant nothing.

"Pretty Tweetie! Pretty Tweetie! Pretty Tweetie!"

The shrill little voice made him miss a step, and he clung to the banisters, shaking. That damn bird, he thought, Helen will really have to . . .

But Helen was dead. She would do nothing about the bird, ever again. Whatever the tiresome problems were, they would be Martin's problems.

He was on the landing now, fumbling with his keys like an old man. It took him ages to get the door open.

What *did* you have to do when someone was dead? Helen would know, or would soon find out. She was good at finding things out for him. She would find out who to phone, what to say to them.

But it was Helen who was dead. She would find out nothing for him, ever again.

He couldn't take it in, the shock was too great. I need a stiff drink, darling, I've just had a most terrible shock: and sitting there in the darkness, he waited for her to bring it to him.

She would never bring him a drink again. She would never bring him anything.

Helen is dead, he told himself yet again, but it still seemed to be beyond his understanding. She would have to explain it to him, in simple words, so that he could grasp it. She would have to comfort him.

Stretched out on the couch, face downwards, he lay in the dark waiting for her arms to come round him.

It had been past midnight when Martin had arrived at the hospital, and they'd told him straight away that she just might survive, though the danger was still great. The stab wound had been perilously near the heart, and she had lost a fearful amount of blood, which was why she might not survive the operation, which was in itself (they assured him) a relatively straightforward one.

"Why don't you go home and get some sleep?" the tired young Registrar suggested. "We'll send for you immediately if —if there's any news."

Martin had heard the hesitation. "If we see she is dying," he had been going to say, but had corrected himself just in time.

"Everything's being done that can be done," the young doctor continued. "Really, Mr. Lockwood, it would be best if you were to go home now, it really would. We could arrange a car . . ."

But Martin just sat there. This small, bare waiting-room, where he had first been told the news, seemed, now, like the only home he had ever known. He could not bring himself to go elsewhere. Two or three people, in the course of the long night, came in to urge him to go and get some sleep, but still he sat on.

Helen might be dead. It was a long time, now, since anyone had come to tell him anything, and this time, the words *did* have meaning. The merciful anaesthesia of shock was wearing M4 off, and he knew, now, exactly what it was that might be coming to him.

Grief. Bereavement. Love. He'd heard these words many a time, and had used them, too, of course. Had used them easily, confidently and in appropriate contexts, all his life long, as a blind man uses verbs of seeing. Now, for the first time, he knew what these words actually stood for.

"You may come now, Mr. Lockwood," said Sister, solid and foursquare in the doorway. "This way, please," and she led the way along corridors, past closed doors, in and out of lifts.

She was taking him to Helen: and there were only two reasons why she would be doing such a thing in the deep dark before dawn. One, that the operation had been successful, and that Helen was recovering consciousness, perhaps asking for him: two, that she was dying, and he was to be allowed to say goodbye.

The cubicle at the far end of the ward was closely curtained: Sister stood, one hand on the edge of the curtain, waiting for him to catch up with her.

Which was it to be? Joy and comfort unspeakable, or grief beyond all comprehending?

But one thing was certain: whichever it was, he would be experiencing it to its ultimate, overwhelming limit: for somehow, during these last hours, he had changed into a person who could feel things: just as other people had been all along.

Celia Fremlin's first novel won an Edgar Award from the Mystery Writers of America. This is her fourteenth novel, and her fourth for the Crime Club. Her previous books include *With No Crying*, *The Spider-Orchid*, and *The Long Shadow*. She lives in London.